FIERY VENGEANCE

The archers let loose their arrows, and there was a scream from one of the attacking ships. The Northmen were nearly upon them. Dec mumbled the enchantment, trying his best to remember the words. He uttered the command word and a bolt of electrical energy surged from his hands. There was a blinding flash followed by a tremendous bang.

But it had gone in the wrong direction. Dec's jaw dropped in amazement. A roar of laughter came from the Northmen.

"What're ya doin'?" screamed the captain. "Strike the foes, not us!"

"Wait, I know what I did wrong," Dec answered breathlessly. This time he said the opposite of the command word he had previously uttered and the bolt of lightning flew straight and true, right into the midst of the closest of the pursuers.

Bodies flew over the side, and after the clap of thunder came the sickening crack of the mast as it fell in flames on the hapless Northmen. The second ship quickly backed oars and turned aside amid the screams of those dying in the fire next to them.

Elfwood

ROSE ESTES

ACE BOOKS, NEW YORK

This book is an Ace original edition,
and has never been previously published.

ELFWOOD

An Ace Book / published by arrangement with
Bill Fawcett and Associates

PRINTING HISTORY
Ace edition / December 1992

Cover art by Erik Olson.

ISBN: 0-441-18376-X

Ace Books are published by The Berkley Publishing Group,
200 Madison Avenue, New York, New York 10016.

PRINTED IN THE UNITED STATES OF AMERICA

10 9 8 7 6 5 4 3 2 1

Special thanks to
Tom Wham
whose contributions and ideas
made this book possible

ELFWOOD

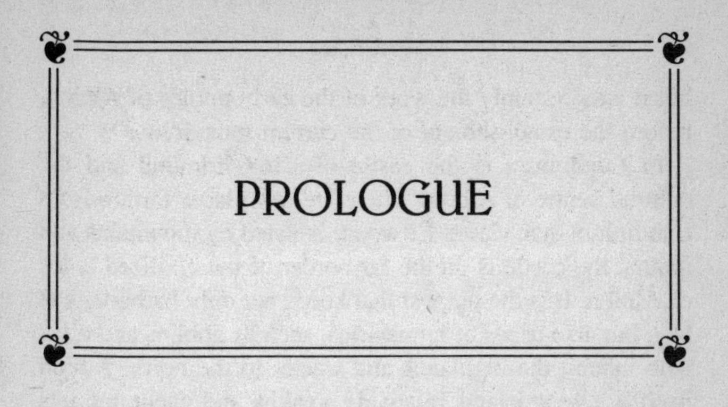

PROLOGUE

IN THE LAND OF ALBION, ASTRIDE A BLUFF, OVERLOOKING THE BROAD River Tyrell, stands Castle Elfwood, more keep than a true castle, by later definition. It is a stone motte and bailey fort with a great hall and many smaller buildings surrounded by a curtain wall. In the distance can be seen the ocean, and when the tide comes in, River Tyrell flows the other direction. Across the river lies the southern border of the Elfwood, the last remaining stand of the land's original forest.

The castle is also situated astride one end of Offa's Wall, built hundreds of years before, to keep out the Northern Barbarians by the last of the Imperial Governors, Offa Sarcassm. The wall, now fallen through disuse, still exists as a raised mound and is now used primarily as a road by those foolish enough to travel along the border.

Castle Elfwood itself dates from several centuries of occasional construction. Much of the base of the wall remains from a permanent Empire camp built during a time of conquest. The Great Hall was built after the empire, and no historian or scholar can be sure when it was constructed, but it was certainly the work of the early nobles of Albion, before the establishment of the current monarchy.

In Lundinium is the castle of King Edmund and the cultural centre of Albion. There are few places farther from Lundinium than Castle Elfwood. Isolated by mountains and moors, the castle is on the far border of the civilized lands of Albion. It is the outpost that keeps not only barbarians at bay, but also tribes of humanoids, such as goblins and orcs, who inhabit the highlands and wastes to the north. Albion itself is a great island, relatively wealthy and intent upon its own affairs. Its rulers have made it a point to stay out of the affairs on the great continent nearby, off the South Coast.

North of Castle Elfwood is the Elfwood itself. Within it dwell the remnants of the earlier forest races and a cult of human Druids and their followers. The Elfwood, a dark and mysterious primal forest, by its very age and nature is magical. Before the humans came, it was home to the elves. It is also the ''soul'' of Albion . . . if lost it would mean an age of ruin for the entire island. Sadly, only the Druids and the Lord of Castle Elfwood know or understand this. These days the border is rife with unrest. The humanoids and the barbarians have risen up in revolt against the order established by the lords of Castle Elfwood. Shortly, the stewardship of Elfwood will change hands, and the fate of Albion hangs in the balance.

Chapter 1

THE TOURNAMENT

THE SMALL GROUP OF HORSEMEN PLODDED SILENTLY ALONG THE forest path, the sound of their hooves muffled by the fallen leaves. Now and again bright rays of morning sunlight filtered through the green of the trees and glistened off the polished armour of the knights. It was the beginning of summer and the forest was fresh and clean. To the rear of the horsemen were four mail-clad pikemen who had fallen somewhat behind so they could talk among themselves without bothering their master. After the men-at-arms came a group of servants leading a string of pack mules that carried all the baggage required to maintain a small band of knights.

The Sixth Lord of Elfwood, Richard Mortimer, paid no notice to the jabbering of his soldiers and squirmed uncomfortably in his saddle. The day was young, yet already the weight of his armour weighed heavily upon him, almost as heavily as did his age, not to mention the responsibilities of his office. Things had grown rather tense on the border lately. The barbarians had found a new leader, Ufa the Bald, who had claimed all the land on both sides of the river as his own. Richard had been forced into an unwelcome alliance with Lord Felker of Harrowhall, to raise an army large enough to drive Ufa back into the highlands.

For the moment there was peace, and today there was to be a great tournament to celebrate the victory. In earlier, happier times, Richard would have looked forward to the festivities and the test of arms. He shook his head slowly and sighed. Perhaps it had been that last battle with the barbarians . . . or was it that night sleeping in the rain on the moor?

"My lord, you look unwell!" came a concerned voice by his side. It was Gardiner, trusted companion and as good a swordsman as there was in all of Albion. "Let us stop and refresh ourselves."

Before he could utter a word, Richard found his companions dismounted and he himself being eased down from his saddle.

"Hands off me!" barked Richard, coming to his senses. "I may be a bit weary, but at least I can still unhorse myself." So saying, he hopped ungracefully to the ground, lost his balance, and fell backward into the grass with a clatter of plate armour. When the string of expletives and laughter had cleared the air, the others helped Lord of Elfwood to his feet.

"I always said you could unhorse the best of them, Richard," remarked Gardiner, handing his master an oilskin of cool water. The knights walked over to a clearing where a fallen log provided seating, and servants appeared with bread and fruit.

"I was wondering, m'lord," said Lewis, the tallest of the company, "just why this tourney has been situated in the clearing by Wycham Wood? 'Tis so remote, there'll be few to witness our deeds of prowess."

Richard shook his head. "'Twas not my doing. This whole affair has been arranged by our erstwhile allies at Harrowhall." He turned to Gardiner. "Have you the parchment we received?" A scroll was produced and Lord of Elfwood held it out for Lewis. "Here, read the details for yourself."

Lewis grinned sheepishly. "Nay, m'lord. 'Twould be naught but a page of chicken scratches to my eyes. My skill is with the sword, not the pen."

"I'll drag you into my library and you'll have book learning forced down your throat!" Richard said, grinning good-naturedly. "It won't do for my men not to be able to read my dispatches." He handed the parchment back to Gardiner. "Anyway, whatever the location of this tournament, I'm certain the representatives of Castle Elfwood gathered here will give the boys from Harrowhall an unpleasant taste of the lance." A low growl of agreement came from those seated beside him on the log.

The meal finished and their lord refreshed, the knights remounted and rode on down the forest trail. Richard was feeling in somewhat better spirits. In truth, the thought of knocking that pompous ass Felker off his horse cheered him considerably.

It was nearly noon when they came out of the woods and rode into the clearing by Wycham Wood. There were several gaily colored tents and a small grandstand erected near the center of the area. The red-and-black flags of Harrowhall waved sullenly in the gentle breeze. Richard led his procession toward the tents.

"M'lord," whispered Gardiner at his side. "Something's amiss."

"Aye!" Richard held up his hand and, as one, the group came to a halt. "Where are our hosts?" He surveyed the scene. The stands were empty; not a person could be seen. There were no boisterous peasants, barking dogs, or screaming children. A smoking fire pit was the only sign of life.

The Sixth Lord of Elfwood nodded and the group edged slowly to the vacant encampment. "Mayhap a bit of magic is afoot, m'lord," offered one of the knights. "This could be an illusion created by the Druids."

"Now, why would they bother with all this?" asked Richard. "More likely the work of Gratten, the Red Mage."

"You mean the slimy toad who works for Felker, m'lord. This is the kind of stunt he would pull. And yet you put yourself at peril by not having a mage to serve you in Castle Elfwood," Gardiner said grimly. They rode forward slowly.

"If it pleases you any, Gardiner," answered Richard with a smile, "I sent word to the Magisterium Lundinium for just such a mage upon our return from the North. I have for too long resisted the practice of magic in Castle Elfwood. When he arrives, we shall see if he proves to be of any use to us."

Gardiner smiled. "A decision I am certain you will not regret m'lord."

Richard stopped his horse next to a tent, pulled out his sword, and sliced one of the ropes with a slash. "'Tis real enough! No magic about that." The tent sagged to one side, then collapsed on itself.

Suddenly Gardiner stood up in his stirrups and stared off into the distance, shading his eyes with his hand. "There's the answer," he said in a low, ominous voice. One of the servants screamed, and the horses grew nervous and danced uncontrollably beneath their riders. Coming out of the woods, spreading in every direction, was an army of pike-armed footmen, clad mostly in black tunics emblazoned with a yellow diamond shape. They were closing in on the small group of knights at a fast walk.

Richard spurred his horse and led his group in a trot around the grandstand. The servants and pikemen ran after as best they could.

"Damnation!" yelled Lewis as they were forced to a halt. "The blackguards are everywhere!

"I don't think they've come for the joust, either." the Lord of Elfwood said in an ironic voice.

"Felker's men, no doubt," ventured Gardiner as he unsheathed his sword.

"I think not," said Richard, who was calmly hoisting his shield up from where it had hung on the saddle. "I've ne'er seen the likes of these ruffians before."

"Perhaps Ufa is getting his revenge," came a voice from the back.

"Men like these would never work for that barbarian." Richard nudged his mount and led his knights, again at a trot, back in the direction from which they had come. "In any case, we're not going to stay around long enough to find out!" He held his sword up high in the air and let out a bloodthirsty battle yell. Gardiner and the others did likewise and the knights of Elfwood fanned out into a wall and then charged into the horde of advancing footmen. Scrambling along behind came the four footmen and the terrified servants who had left their pack mules behind.

In the face of the unexpected charge, the front ranks of the black-clad footmen dropped their weapons and tried to flee. But there was no place for them to run, for their numbers were great and the closing circle of armed men pressed inexorably forward. Richard and his knights smashed into the mass, and the one-sided battle was joined. Steel rang against steel as the mounted killing machines that were the knights carved their way through the men on foot—to a point. Then the black army, ignoring the horrible casualties it was suffering, swarmed over the band of valiant knights. One by one they were dragged off their mounts and disappeared into the tangle of the battle.

In just a few minutes it was all over, and the field fell silent save for the cries of the wounded. Under the shady branches of a large tree at the edge of the clearing, three dark figures on horseback had observed the carnage from a position of safety. Two were clad in the same black armour as that of the murderous army.

"Very well executed, I'd say," said the first dark figure proudly.

"Some of your men ran. I'll have their heads."

"Your word is my command. I shall attend to it at once, master." The first figure spurred his horse and rode out into the clearing.

"Just the same, you have earned your reward," said the third figure, in a low snarl. "This pleases me." He snapped his fingers, and three servants came out of the bushes carrying heavy bags of coins which they laboriously draped across the saddle of the dark warrior's horse.

Chapter 2

THE SEVENTH LORD

THE POLISHED AXE FELL FURIOUSLY, CLEAVING A FOOT-LONG CHUNK of wood which flew through the air like a missile. Another blow was struck and more splinters flew. Those who had been standing nearby suddenly took notice and began to back away. It was obvious that the young master was in one of his moods. Jaeme, son of Richard, Lord of Elfwood, had channeled all his rage into the muscles of his arms and the blade in his hands. Why had he been left behind on the frontier after Ufa had fled? *Chop*! This duty was beneath the dignity of the son of the Lord of Elfwood! *Whack!*

Keeping watch over a village of miserable peasants with scarcely a pitchfork among them! *Whack! Crunch!* The log broke into two parts, one of which fell to the ground with a thump. Jaeme dropped his axe, sighed, and wiped the sweat from his brow with the back of his hand.

The future Lord of Elfwood was tall for his age, and still a bit on the awkward side. Yet he had mastered the skills of battle and been knighted by King Edmund at the royal castle in Lundinium over a year ago. His straight Roman nose made him quite popular among the ladies of the court, but the feature they liked most were his dark brown, almost-black eyes. Without knowing it, when Jaeme stared at someone, his striking countenance commanded attention.

He was clad in buckskins today. Jaeme eschewed armour whenever possible; it restricted his freedom of movement, and, as he had proved in the recent battle with Ufa's barbarians, it gave him a quickness not attainable by armoured knights.

Ufa was far away, making plans no doubt, but in the distant highlands. His supporters had been scattered to the far winds by Richard and the armies of Elfwood and their allies. Now Jaeme wondered long and hard why he was still here in the highlands, protecting against a defeated enemy. At least the tiny village of Ahtska was pleasant enough, situated as it was near a large pine wood and adjacent to a clear mountain stream in the foothills. And the villagers considered the troops from the south to be their saviours. Ufa had not treated them well, having murdered many of the men and carried off a considerable number of the women.

Just then, one of his boon companions, Joseph, stumbled into his field of view, proudly holding an enormous earthenware jug from which he had obviously already partaken. He wobbled forward and sat down heavily on the log next to his friend.

"Phew! Jaeme, this cost me ten ducats, but I swear, the brew is worth it!" Joseph proffered the bottle, and the future Earl of Elfwood, who had worked up quite a thirst flailing away at the log, accepted with a bow and a grin. He took a long draught and immediately regretted it, for the mixture was thick and aromatic. He screwed up his face and gurgled, barely managing to swallow. It burned all the way down.

"Phew!" Jaeme choked. "Great stuff—" He gasped for

breath and continued in a raspy whisper. ''Perhaps a wee bit''—gulp—''strong.''

Joseph Willoughby laughed. Grabbing the jug, he hoisted it over his shoulder in time-honored tradition and partook. Willoughby was the son of one of the poorer nobles in the lands surrounding Castle Elfwood. He was the same age as Jaeme, and the two had become fast friends years ago, when they were both entered as squires-at-arms on the same day and began their training to become knights of the realm. In a stand-up fight—with wooden swords, of course—Joseph was Jaeme's better. But armed with a wooden mace or axe, Jaeme was the master. Together, they thought of themselves as the perfect fighting team.

The effects of the jug were soon felt, and the two were presently joined by the other knights remaining in this barbarian backwater village, located on the southern bounds of the highlands. The local brew was strong enough to wipe out five of the youngest knights of Elfwood . . . and when they had passed out, it claimed two men-at-arms, who had gladly inherited the remains of Joseph's jug.

Jaeme awoke to the sound of a cock crowing. He lay sprawled out beneath a tree, his legs draped over Joseph, who was snoring loudly beside him. The future Earl of Elfwood groaned and lifted himself up on his elbows. His head ached and his body was stiff, and once again he wished he had stuck to his resolve not to drink so much. He struggled to his feet, picked his way through the sprawl of men passed out around him, and stumbled down to the stream. At the bank he pondered the idea of jumping in with his clothes on, but the thought of wet buckskins chafing all day had no appeal. He sat down clumsily on a grassy hummock and slowly removed all his garments. At length he was naked and plunged into the icy stream with a shout.

The ruckus he made, splashing about and yelping in the frigid water, soon gained the attention of his youthful squire, Skyler, who came running with a large cloth to towel down his master when he emerged from the stream. Some of the others who had suffered the effects of the jug were slowly making their way down to the water, and the smell of cooking came from the camp.

As Jaeme emerged from his bath and dried himself, he felt infinitely better but for the ache which still nagged at his head. He hoped there would be no trouble today, but he was not too worried; all had been calm here for over a week.

Later, the sun was well up in the sky, and Jaeme and his companions were seated at the long table by the fire breaking the fast. The talk was subdued, as many present had suffered the same fate as their master.

Then the riders appeared. There were two of them, and they rode up over the crest of the hill and down toward the camp at a full gallop. Dogs began barking and men jumped for their weapons.

"This could be trouble," Jaeme whispered under his breath to nobody in particular, dropping a crust of bread to the table. He put his hand to his aching forehead and frowned as he rose slowly to his feet. If this was trouble, he was in no condition for battle.

But, as the riders came nearer, the emblems of Elfwood became apparent on their clothing. They reined in the lathered horses, and the taller of the two hopped down and rushed forward to the table. Jaeme recognized him; it was one of the huntsmen from the castle. The young man looked weary and unshaven. He had obviously ridden all night.

The messenger stopped before Jaeme and knelt down on

one knee before him, taking a moment to catch his breath. At last he looked up and spoke.

"Dire news, m'lord," uttered the huntsman in a sad, breathless voice. "Your father, Lord Richard . . ." He hesitated. Tears filled his eyes. "Your father has been ambushed . . . murdered."

The trip back to Castle Elfwood was a long, sad affair for Jaeme. He, Joseph, and his closest companions had ridden on ahead. The seventh Lord of Elfwood had bidden the rest of the force to break camp and return home as quickly as possible. He rode at the head of the column, stone-faced, silent, and oblivious to the beautiful cloudless day and the vibrant greens of the forests through which they passed.

The grave news, compounded by the hangover caused by his foolish behaviour the night before, filled his mind with fears and doubts. He was not fit or ready to assume the mantle of responsibility that came with the office of Lord of Elfwood. Then Jaeme's thoughts focused on those responsible for the death of his father, and he seethed with rage. He would have his revenge . . . but how? And who could have done such a thing? The young lord clenched his teeth and sighed. He was not ready for this at all.

The great courtyard, or lower bailey of Castle Elfwood was filled with several great mounds of wood. Each of the pyres was covered with dark bunting, and atop each pile was a group of dead knights, resplendent in their polished armour. Surmounting the tallest pile of wood was the body of Richard, Sixth Lord of Elfwood. Flowers hung from his pyre in abundance, and the many hundreds of onlookers milling about below were weeping audibly at the sight of their former master.

Jaeme, his face locked in a frown, came out the door of the upper hall, crossed the balcony, and faced the crowd. Behind him came in local prelate, the Archbishop of Umbria, and several of the local lords, including Felker, and most of the castle staff. Jaeme raised his hand and all fell silent. He then stepped aside and the Archbishop began his rather lengthy eulogy in a loud, clear voice—so loud, in fact, that those with him on the balcony winced in pain at some of his more booming expressions.

Jaeme stood back and let his eyes wander, not listening to the words that were ringing so loudly in his ears. The great funeral pyre was at once more than he had expected and less than he had hoped for. All those times Jaeme had given his father grief, or been contrary just for the sake of being contrary, came back to haunt him now. Tears welled up in his eyes—for his father, and the others, all those fine men he had come to know and love, the knights who had taught him so much, the knights who had surrounded his father. And now they were all dead, dead by the hand of some unknown person or force. Now he was alone and they would advise him no more. Well, not quite alone. Beside him stood Polonius, the master-at-arms.

But even old Polonius had not been much comfort. Since the murder, which the master-at-arms blamed squarely on himself for not being with Richard when he was needed most, the man had refused to speak to anyone. Jaeme sighed and wondered if he was fit to become the Earl of Elfwood.

His gaze turned to the local nobles and he fixed on Lord Felker, a man he despised. Had the short fat master of Harrowhall not been out hunting on the day of the ambush, and been attacked and wounded by a wild boar—or so he said—he would have been Jaeme's prime suspect as the architect of his father's murder. Yet Felker stood there with a tear in his eye, and he had brought many gifts and offerings of goodwill. Jaeme was perplexed.

Just then the Archbishop finished his eulogy and a group of ladies from the castle began to sing a sad song. The fires were lit and the kindling took to flame. Soon, billowing clouds of black smoke rose to the sky. The heat burned Jaeme's face and he turned away. Someday he would avenge his father. He would find the murderers and do unto them what they had done to his family. . . .

Chapter 3

DECUTONIUS CONSULUS

THE WIZENED OLD MAGE TURNED TO ADDRESS HIS AUDIENCE, WHICH consisted of a collection of the most promising young magic users in all of Albion. "Now, I add this powder to the mixture," he said, holding up a small cloth bag. "'Tis Pylaxus root. Don't confuse it with Pyreon powder, or the thing will explode in your face."

The grey-bearded teacher turned back to his experiment, which consisted of an iron pot bubbling over a small fire in the centre of the room. The room was warm and dark, as were many of the rooms at the Magisterium. Owing to the fire and the smoke, it was hard to breathe, let alone pay attention to the lecture. The students were, to a varying degree, not really paying attention but busying themselves with other things. One was scribbling funny pictures on a sheet of parchment; another was attempting to roll a gold coin back and forth between his fingers without dropping it; two young ladies in the back were discussing an amorous adventure; and two others had fallen asleep. Only one of the pupils, Dec, seemed truly intent upon the lesson at hand. He had been paying close attention to every word Old Squintum had to say, and now suddenly he dropped out of his chair and hid under a table against the wall. Dec knew what was about to happen. A little bag of Pyreon powder fell out of his clothing and landed with a puff on the stone floor. He quickly snatched it up and hid it inside his shirt.

Decutonius Consulus, or Dec as he was known to his friends, son of Dunboyne Consulus, commissioner to the Crown had, from his very birth, shown great potential as a magic user, for the Consulus family tree contained a long line of magically gifted wizards. As a baby, without training, he mastered the art of levitating himself out of his crib and onto the carpets, where he then proceeded to get into all sorts of mischief. His mother had insisted that he follow in the footsteps of his venerable ancestors and pursue a career in magic.

Yet now Dec was in his early twenties and still had not become a licensed mage. At first his father had tried live-in tutors, but Dec's lack of a sense of purpose, and worse, his rather pointed sense of humor, had driven them all away. He had been sent to Portia to study under the great mage Mutimer, only to be sent home a year later, having destroyed a wing of the local castle as the result of a prank.

Now Dec was in his second year at the Lundinium Magisterium, and how he had survived that long was more a testament to the political clout of his father than to his attentiveness to his studies. His practical jokes had alienated just about all of the instructors, and now he was about to try the patience of Old Squintum, the last of the lot who thought Dec had any future in the field.

The two girls in the back suddenly took notice of Dec's actions, knowing full well what they meant. They passed the word around the classroom, and soon even the two sleeping students had been awakened and all had taken cover behind benches and overturned tables. All this commotion went unnoticed by the instructor, who droned on about the fine points of measuring out the correct amount of powdered Pylaxus root. At last he pulled a little spoon out of one of his pockets and dipped it into the bag, measuring out three full spoons into the boiling pot.

"There, now we will let it simmer for a few minutes before pouring it into the flask . . . and . . . What?" Squintum had turned back to face his students and raised his eyebrows as he discovered they had all taken cover. First, a look of consternation crossed his face; then his eyes widened at the significance of what he saw before him. There was a pregnant moment of silence, before he dropped the spoon to the stone floor. It bounced twice.

"Decutonius!" he yelled at the top of his voice as he fell flat on the floor and covered his head. Fortunately, the iron pot channeled the force of the subsequent explosion up toward the roof, pieces of which were blown halfway across Lundinium.

Later that afternoon Dec and his worried father stood in the hall outside the door of the Wizard of Lundinium. Dunboyne Consulus, a short, worried-looking man, pulled on his prematurely grey hair and frowned at his son.

"Decutonius, you'll be the death of me and your poor mother, yet! How could you have done such a thing?"

"Well, I didn't realize Old Squintum was going to put in three spoons—"

"That has nothing to do with the issue here!" interrupted his father. "The point is that you would even attempt such a foolish thing. King Edmund himself has spoken to me about this matter." He crossed his hands behind his back and began pacing back and forth. "You are here for a deep and serious purpose, not to play pranks and jokes." Dunboyne stopped and looked at his son, who was staring absently out the window, apparently not listening to a word he had been saying.

''Dec!''

''I am paying attention Father. I was just watching this little spider build its web.'' Dec pointed to the upper corner of the window. ''It's a regular work of art.''

His father growled something unintelligible, pulled at his hair again, and resumed pacing back and forth. Dec always managed to do this to him.

Just then the Wizard's immense oak door squeaked open and a servant dressed in a red robe came out into the hall.

''The Wizard will see you now.'' They were led into a huge stone room, with great hewn timbers supporting the roof. The walls were covered with tapestries depicting famous events from the history of both the Empire and that of the Monarchy of Albion. Dec stared at the hangings in awe, for he had never been in the Wizard's private chambers before. They were led to the far side of the room, where the Great Wizard sat behind a large thick slate table, flanked on either side by the instructors of the Magisterium Lundinium. None of them were smiling. Dec slouched as he walked, attempting to become as invisible as possible. The servant seated them on a low bench before the table, and the Wizard and his companions seemed to tower over Dec and his father.

''Good Master Dunboyne Consulus,'' began the Wizard. ''I am very sorry to have drawn you into this matter. Under ordinary conditions we would have communicated with you via the post.'' He leaned forward and scowled, his bushy black eyebrows nearly covering his eyes. ''But this is not an ordinary condition!'' There was a murmur of agreement from the faculty seated near him.

Dec, who thus far had been paying as little attention as possible to the proceedings, now noticed that one of the instructors, the one who hated him most, was making rapid hand gestures under his clock, out of the Wizard's sight. Dec had seen such gestures before. They were the passes pursuant to a mind-control spell.

Dec was suddenly worried. He couldn't allow this to happen to his father or the school would soak him for everything the Consulus family owned. Keeping his own hands low, where they also could not easily be seen, Dec began gesturing a counterspell. Meanwhile, the Wizard droned on, listing all the incidents and problems caused by Dec in his year and a half at the Magisterium. Fortunately, the accused was concentrating on the counterspell and did not hear the sordid details about his long list of crimes.

"Now, as for the results of today's explosion—" The Mage unrolled a scroll and read from it. "The entire roof of the classroom wing will have to be replaced at a cost of five thousand two hundred and fifty-three crowns, five shillings and sixpence." Dunboyne's face went white.

The Wizard cleared his throat and continued. "It was a miracle that no one was killed, but several passers-by were wounded by falling debris. They are making damage claims against the Magisterium of approximately another two thousand crowns. Estimates on cleanup costs have not come in yet, but I'd say they'll run you another hundred crowns, easy."

"We . . . I shall gladly pay for the damages, of course," said Dec's father in a tense, raspy voice, tugging at his hair nervously. "And please accept my sincerest apologies—"

"I'm not finished yet," interrupted the Wizard. Dec noticed that the instructor upon whom he had been working the counterspell now sat glassy-eyed, unmoving, staring into space. Next to him sat Old Squintum, who had been watching the little interplay. He winked knowingly at Dec and nodded with a smile. At least Squintum was still his friend.

''It is the decision of the majority of the senior magicians here at the Magisterium, that your son, Decutonius will never successfully become a Mage of the First Order.'' Dec winced and his father began pulling at his hair again.

''He has shown little propensity toward serious application of the knowledge imparted to him by his elders and has repeatedly subjected the members of our faculty to humiliating pranks and tricks which he must somehow, in a perverted fashion, think funny. Well, we are not of the same mind. It is the decision of the majority that Decutonius Consulus be hereby dismissed from the Magisterium Lundinium!''

''But, but . . .'' was all Dec's father could manage to say. Dec, meanwhile, squirmed uneasily on the bench. How could he have done this?

''However,'' continued the Wizard, ''owing to your high standing in the court of King Edmund, and the long and honorable tradition of accomplished wizardry in your family, we have decided to give your son one LAST chance.'' Solemnly, the Wizard stood up. Leaning forward, he rested both hands on the table and stared directly at Dec.

''We have here''—he held up a short bit of parchment—''a request from the Earl of Elfwood for a mage.'' Dec's eyes widened at this revelation. Elfwood? Where in Albion was Elfwood?

''It is with great reluctance that I am giving you this assignment, for you certainly do not deserve it.'' The

Wizard banged his fist on the table, but as it was made of stone, the gesture had little effect.

"Were it not for the recommendation of Master Mage Squintum, I would be throwing you out on your ear instead." He sat back down with an expression of defeat. "As it is, Elfwood is as far away as I can possibly send you. I now have my doubts as to the safety of the frontiers of Albion with you on the border." He picked up a small scroll tied neatly with golden string. "You will go with the rank of Apprentice. God help the Lord of Elfwood. He will need it."

Dec timidly grasped the scroll, and the Wizard sat down with a thump. The interview was obviously over, and he and his father rose and hurried quickly out the door, which opened mysteriously at their approach.

"Where is Castle Elfwood, Father?" asked Dec, studying the scroll as they walked down the stair.

His father shook his head mumbled to himself for a moment, then answered. "A long way to the north, I fear. But probably not far enough."

Chapter 4

AN UNWELCOME HONOR

The Druids of the Elfwood were an ancient and mysterious people, whose love of nature and in particular the Elfwood itself, transcended all else. Their origins went back beyond pre-Empire times, but even the Empire was never able to take control of the wood and its inhabitants. Through the centuries, the Druids had used their wiles and their magics to repel one invader after another. With the rise of the Monarchy of Albion, Druid elders arranged a truce, and since that time, a shaky but stable alliance had existed between the worshippers of the mystical woods and the monarchy based in Lundinium.

The key to the truce rested in the hands of the master of Castle Elfwood, who for generations had pledged to uphold and preserve the ancient and treasured wood, named for the elves who once made it their home. There were many forces who coveted and would undo the primeval forest. Chief among those forces, and most mindless of all, was the growing human population, expanding ever northward into the frontiers. Farmers on all sides of the wood were ever in quest of new lands to till, and, more important, lesser nobles in the borderlands saw the apparent wilderness of the Elfwood as a natural place in which to expand their holdings.

Now Richard Mortimer, staunch defender of the primal forest was dead, and the Druids faced a crisis. His son, still a teenager, had assumed the title and duties of the steward of Castle Elfwood, and the druidical elders were worried. The boy, a virtual unknown to them, by all reports had spent most of his childhood in frivolous pursuit of material pleasures, and his attention to the duties of knighthood came only second to him. Only last year, on his twenty-first birthday, was the young lord knighted.

Something had to be done. A special meeting of the grand council was called. They met in the highest places among the tallest, oldest trees. There, over the years, the branches had been persuaded to grow into the shapes of rooms and corridors, like most of the habitations of the forest Druids, through the pervasive magic indigenous to their race.

The meeting was stormy, and many opinions were voiced. The council argued nonstop for over thirty hours, and the net result was that an ambassador must be sent to reaffirm the age-old understanding between the Druids of Elfwood and the newest steward of the castle.

Laelestequenstrutia (known usually as Laela to her friends) glumly pondered the summons she had received. When the elders called, you had no choice but to come . . . but usually when the elders called, it was for some distasteful project they had dreamed up, one they would never consider doing themselves, and now they had decided to lay the burden upon one of the younger Druids . . . in this case Laela. She rolled over slowly in her bed of dry leaves and again studied the words scrawled on the parchment, hoping to find a different meaning than the one she knew was real: Laela, you are summoned to deal with marauding dragons . . . Laela, you are summoned to change the course of the river Tyrell and stop the spring flooding . . . Laela, your services are required at the court of King Edmund in Lundinium. Please report to the court of King Edmund immediately.

"Rats!" she exclaimed and sat up on the edge of the bed.

Lewtt, the wood sprite, who had been standing upon Laela's toes, flew into the air unceremoniously and crashed into a tree branch, clinging to it for dear life. A four-inch-tall wood sprite is something forgotten by its mistress.

Despite her vivid imagination, the words on the scroll remained unchanged. She was to appear before the grand council at her earliest convenience. Which meant now. Lewtt regained his senses, dropped down from the branch in which he hung feet first, and took to wing, hovering just in front of Laela's nose.

"Oh! My sweet pet!" she held out her hand and Lewtt settled softly upon her smooth fingers. "I am so sorry. I forgot about you completely. You're not hurt, are you?" The two communicated telepathically, but Laela always vocalized her speech to him. Lewtt answered in the quiet voice that spoke directly to her mind.

My lady, your fits will be my undoing . . . yet there is no one alive today as beautiful as you. A feeling of warmth and love flowed out from the little sprite and into Laela. She enjoyed it and then shook her head in amazement. Just who was in charge here? Was this sprite her servant, or was she just his enormous slave?

He read her thoughts and smiled knowingly at her. Laela frowned petulantly. That didn't answer her question. Laela was quite beautiful by any standards, although she failed to think of herself in that way. Her head was surrounded by a halo of curly red hair which glowed magnificently in the sunlight that streamed in through the branches above, and her emerald green eyes were inherited from her grandfather, who she was told came from the lands of the Northmen.

Methinks the only way to discern the meaning of your summons is to proceed posthaste unto the trees of the council, said Lewtt, as he landed softly on her shoulder.

"I know, I know!" she complained. Laela stood up and shooed the sprite from her shoulder, then pulled off her simple green frock and stood naked. She muttered an incantation and her body seemed to dissolve, and where a moment before there had stood a beautiful young maiden, there was now a red-plumed falcon, stretching and testing its wings. A wise old Druidess named Myrna, a friend of her long-dead mother, had taught Laela how to change herself into any one of several forest animals. For long trips in this primal wood, nothing could beat the speed and directness of the flight of a falcon.

"Let's be off," said the girl/falcon in a curious combination of chirps and squawks, but Lewtt understood clearly, and followed at his best speed as the falcon soared skyward with a flutter of wings.

Laela rose quickly above the treetops and climbed steadily higher. In the back of her mind she could hear Lewtt complaining, as he always did when she flew so high into the air. She ignored him, for to fly in this way was exhilarating, and the girl often wished she could remain a falcon indefinitely. But the spell would wear off all too soon and she had better be near the earth when that happened. All the more reason for her to take the beginning of any flight at the highest possible altitude.

She caught a thermal, stopped flapping, and joyfully

circled with her wings outstretched, climbing even higher thanks to the wind. At length the gust departed and she leveled off and began coasting in the direction of the council trees. Lewtt, who dared not leave the protection of the forest cover, skimmed the treetops below his mistress, flying now as fast as he could to keep up.

Within minutes, a beautiful falcon soared under the archway of branches that formed the entrance of the council tree complex. The two eagles who stood watch at the gate knew her well enough and took no notice as Laela flashed past them into the darkness of the interior. A moment later there was a naked girl standing inside a small anteroom off the main hall. Laela kept clothing tucked in many nooks and crannies around the forest, especially in those places to which she flew with any regularity. She pulled a soft frock out of the crook of a tree limb just as Lewtt arrived, and with his help, pulled it down over her shoulders.

She made her way barefoot down the uneven floor of the hall, which, like the chambers' walls and roof, was constructed from the carefully aligned branches of many living trees. Arched window openings along the sides let in light and fresh air. Laela always admired this place, for it was the most finely formed work of the Druids, and had taken centuries to grow to this peak of perfection.

She passed two glum-looking figures clad in long robes, who were walking slowly, reading from scrolls as they went. Their faces were hidden by the great hoods they wore and they paid no attention to Laela. She turned through a low door and crossed an open bridge between two trees. The bridge, also made of living branches, was surrounded by luxurious green foliage and was quite cheerful compared to the dark hall she had just left.

At the far end of the bridge was another room, and over

its entrance was fastened a wicker door which opened noiselessly at her approach. This was one of the many council subchambers. It was open and airy, but the mood inside was anything but cheerful. Seated in a semicircle atop a similarly curved raised branch were three very sour-looking old men also clad in long, hooded robes. Their faces were painted purple and they were all frowning at her. Laela stopped just inside the door.

Zooks! What a basket of onions, commented Lewtt silently into her mind. The sprite was seated cross-legged in her hair. She quite agreed with him.

"Laelestequenstrutia, daughter of Styrenestiqua," began the oldest of the three men. His voice was hardly more than a whisper and his dour countenance had not changed. "You have been chosen by the council, ahem, ah . . . not for your skills, for you yet have much to learn, but for your, ahem, your, ah . . . beauty." He had trouble getting the last word out, obviously just seeing that attribute for the first time. His expression brightened a bit and the old man continued, disclosing the mission to which she had been assigned.

Laela rolled her eyes but managed to keep silent as the news of her diplomatic assignment to Castle Elfwood was explained.

"You will serve in the court of the, ah, ahem . . . new lord of the castle, to ensure continued protection for the Elfwood and the greater benefit of all parties concerned." The council Druid talked on, but Laela was not listening. This was the last thing in the world she had imagined her life would come to. Duty in the court of the pimple-faced idiot, Jaeme . . . She had met him only once, thirteen years ago, at the Feast of Quirxmas. He had pulled her hair and run away laughing like a fool. Laela remembered, and had no desire to meet the silly boy—well, now he was a man—ever again.

At last the elder finished speaking, reached under the branch upon which he was seated, and produced an armload of parchment scrolls and a small bag of gold. Laela stepped forward silently and took them in her arms.

"Your arrival has been announced, so they will be expecting you three nights hence. Ahem, now get your affairs in order. This assignment may be a long one." The old man finally broke into what could be misconstrued as a smile, as did the others by his side. Laela turned and left the room without ever having said a word and glumly pondered her newly ordained future.

Chapter 5

THE TRIP NORTH

DECUTONIUS LOOKED ROUND HIS ROOM ONE LAST TIME, HOPING HE hadn't forgotten anything, for it would be a long time before he came home again. He felt pretty bad about sticking his father with all those bills, yet the old man had taken it fairly well, and Dec had only been lectured on the subject ten or fifteen times since. Somehow, he thought, this time would be different. This time he was nobody's student—he was on his own, a real magic-user, albeit as an apprentice, but a magic-user nonetheless. He was going to sink or swim on this one. The thought made him a bit nervous.

Dec spotted a small black book lying on its side at the far end of a bookshelf. In it were the notes he had taken while studying at Portia. It was a good thing he'd found it, for he'd really learned a lot there under Mutimer. It was there he had perfected his skills at counterspells and magic detection. He carefully slipped the book into a pocket on his vest.

"Dec, are you ready?" called his mother. "The coach is here."

"Coming, Mum!" This was it. He lifted the canvas bag with his belongings over his shoulder and shut the door to his room for the last time. He said goodbye to each creaky wooden stair as he made his way down to the entry hall. His mother stood at the bottom of the stair with open arms and a tear in her eye.

"Give me a kiss," she said softly. "You will write to me? Goodness, the frontier is so far away and so dangerous."

"Of course I'll write, and I can take care of myself. You'll see." There was more confidence in his words than in his heart. Dunboyne stopped him as he stepped outside, and shook his hand.

"Take care, son, and do be careful. You've pushed your luck about as far as you can."

"I know, Father. Thank you for squaring things with the Magisterium. Someday soon I shall be able to repay you."

"You have enough money?"

"More than enough. You are too kind." Dec turned and hopped lightly down the steps, as he had done when he was very young. The coachman took his bag and stuffed it into the back of the coach, which looked more like a converted freight wagon with false side panels and a canvas top. Dec climbed in just the same, and barely had he sat down on the hard wooden bench when there was a crack of the whip and the coach jerked and was off with a clatter down the cobblestone street.

Dec was bouncing and jouncing most uncomfortably, as the driver seemed to be in an awful hurry. Then a bit of inspiration came to him, and he practiced his oldest and best bit of magic, levitation. With a minimum of concentration, he rose six inches above the jolting board seat. Then the coach turned a corner, and he promptly banged into the side with his elbow. Quickly, he grabbed the leather straps that hung on either side and stabilized himself in the middle, safely away from floor, roof, and sides. He was more comfortable, but glad that this was only a trip to the docks. Travel by coach to Castle Elfwood would have taken him a fortnight. His father owned a ship that would have him there in two days if the wind was fair, and if they didn't run into any pirates or Northmen.

There was little worry of either these days, as the growing strength of Albion had driven back the Northmen so that now they made only sporadic attacks and these against the wild lands north of Offa's Wall. King Edmund was fond of ships and the sea and had built an impressive navy. This navy had virtually cleared the seas of pirates, and a new and flourishing coastal trade had sprung up all round Albion, and even to the lands beyond.

The ship was called the *Goshawk*, and she was longer and taller than Dec had imagined, with a great castlelike structure at the bow and an even larger one at the stern. The deck was covered with boxes and bags of goods being shipped north, and workmen were busy hauling more on board. He was greeted by the captain, who was called Bottinius, a thick-set, heavily tanned man with silver hair. Dec was given a tiny cabin with a window, high in the stern castle. There was a table that swung down on leather hinges from the wall and a small wood plank that doubled as a seat and a bed. A sailor brought him a straw mattress and a blanket. Dec frowned when he tried to lie down and discovered he was a foot longer than his bunk.

They left with the tide that evening, and at first Dec was quite happy, having never been to sea before. But soon after dark the *Goshawk* rounded the point off Sanctium, and things changed as the ship began to pitch and roll with the sea swell.

Had it been daylight, Dec would have appeared noticeably green to any onlookers. But it was dark and he was alone, and he had forgotten completely about the conjuring trick he had used in the bouncing wagon earlier that day. So he stuck his head out his window and was miserable till, at last, just before dawn, he managed to fall into a fitful sleep.

The captain invited him to breakfast, and Dec decided it would be best not to refuse, though the thought of food made him ill. As he sat down to eat, Bottinius smiled knowingly, for Dec's eyes were red from lack of sleep, his clothes were wrinkled and soiled, and he still had a tinge of green about him. He managed only to drink a cup of water and eat a small biscuit, then returned to his cabin and slept till noon. By then he felt better, his body having adjusted somewhat to the rhythmic motions of ship and sea. The wind was indeed fair, and the captain expected that they would arrive early if the breeze held.

That evening they were passing between a long, tree-covered island and the mainland. The wind had died down considerably, the sea was calm, and the ship was creeping along. Decutonius stood enjoying the gentle breeze on the after castle when he noticed several hands climbing to the top of the mast. He walked over to the captain.

''Hawk Island?'' asked Dec. He had been studying the maps and charts.

''Aye, that it is. A regular haven for pirates, that island, with all its coves and inlets!'' said Bottinius, pointing to the long stretch of land that loomed off to starboard. ''More'n once I've had a close scrape in these waters.''

''Surely they're all gone now?'' said Dec, suddenly a little nervous.

''Aye, thanks to good King Edmund's navy . . . that is, most of 'em.'' He squinted and carefully scanned the horizon. ''There's still one or two what hasn't been caught and brought to justice yet.'' Dec immediately began searching the ocean for pirates, too.

Later, there was a brief stir as they crossed paths with a pair of small luggers, which happily turned out to be friendly fishing boats. The captain bought part of their catch, and the *Goshawk* sailed on. Presently it was dark, and still no pirates, so Dec went below to his tiny cabin to catch up on the sleep he had missed the night before. It took him a while to get comfortable in a space that was twelve inches short, but he finally managed to bend himself in the middle with both feet hanging off the end of the bunk. He soon fell fast asleep.

This restful interlude was not to last very long. Only a few hours later Dec was rudely awakened by shouts and the tramp of feet on the deck above him. He sat up abruptly and bumped his head on the deck beam. When he recovered his senses he glanced out his window, and there, in the moonlight, he could just make out two ghostly shapes with long rows of oars flashing in the water on either side. Two ships were rapidly coming up behind them.

Dec stumbled out of his cabin in the dark, felt his way to the ladder, and climbed up to the top of the after castle. There, a jumble of sailors was leaning over the rail speculating as to the nature of their pursuers. Just then the captain arrived.

''What is it? What's going on here?'' he bellowed.

''It's pirates, Cap'n,'' answered the man at the rudder.

''No, 'tis Northmen,'' said another. ''I see'd 'em before, an' look at them snake heads on the bows.''

The captain took a look for himself. ''Northmen, they are, dammit! To arms, men! To arms!'' The sailors dispersed hastily, sliding down ropes and jumping down ladders, and disappeared into the ship. Dec was now more than a little worried, for he had seen no more than twenty men aboard the *Goshawk*, and the ships of the Northmen had at least that many oars to a side.

As Dec stood dumbfounded, not sure what to do next, Bottinius walked over to him. He put his arm on the young mage's shoulder and looked him square in the eye. ''M'boy, yer father told me ye were some kind of a wizard?''

''Yes.'' One word was all Dec could squeeze out.

''Well, if ye can do somthin' to stop these blackguards I'll be advisin' ye to do it now, or they'll have us sure as yer born.''

''Oh, ah, of course!'' Dec scratched his head, desperately trying to think of something useful he could do, but his mind was a blank. What had he done to destroy the castle at Portia? The book! But wait, that was no good—he couldn't read it by moonlight.

He began pacing in a little circle. It had been a form of lightning that had gone awry. Did he have the material components? Dec made a quick mental inventory of everything he had packed in his bag. Just maybe, he thought. He stopped pacing and quickly went back down the ladder, feeling his way back to his room.

Once again he banged his head on the beam, then began fumbling anxiously through his bag in the dim patch of moonlight that filtered in through his window. He glanced out at the ships, which loomed so close now that he could hear the Northmen chanting as they bent to their oars. The very sound raised the hairs at the back of his neck.

Way down at the bottom of the bag—of course—he found what he wanted, a small piece of amber. He grabbed that and a woolen sock and made his way back up on deck.

The sailors had returned as well, now armed with an assortment of pikes, axes, and swords. Some had even donned helmets. Up in the rigging of the mast he saw three men with longbows, their feet hooked around invisible ropes, already taking aim at the enemy. ''Please stand aside,'' Dec called to the crew. They all shifted quickly to the other half of the stern castle and the apprentice mage stood alone, bracing himself against the rail as the ship rolled gently with the swell.

The archers let loose their arrows, and there was a scream from one of the attacking ships. The Northmen were nearly upon them. Dec mumbled the enchantment, trying his best to remember the words . . . it had been so long ago. He began rubbing the bit of amber with the wool and he felt a tingling in his arms. Something was happening. He uttered the command word, and a bolt of electric energy surged from his hands. There was a blinding flash followed by a tremendous bang.

But it had gone in the wrong direction. The stern castle of the *Goshawk* was partially blown away and the rest was in flames. Dec's jaw dropped open in amazement. A roar of laughter came from the Northmen.

''What're ya doin'?'' screamed the captain. ''Strike the foes, not us!''

''Wait, I know what I did wrong,'' Dec answered breathlessly. He'd made the same mistake at Portia. While Bottinius ordered all of his men aft to fight the fire, Dec once again began to utter the enchantment and began rubbing on the amber. This time he said the opposite of the command word he had previously uttered and the bolt of lighting flew straight and true, right into the midst of the closest of the pursuers.

Bodies flew over the side, and after the clap of thunder came the sickening crack of the mast as it fell in flames on the hapless Northmen. The second ship quickly backed oars and turned aside amid the screams of those dying in the fire next to them.

Dec, however, had worked up quite a fighting frenzy and he was not about to let them get away. Once again he began chanting and rubbing and, quick as a wink, a second bolt of lightning arced across the water and blew the stern completely off the fleeing vessel. It immediately began to sink, and its snakelike nose rose high out of the water like some great monster in the throes of death.

A cheer went up from the archers in the rigging and the two men left at the rudder. The captain and the rest of the crew were too busy fighting their own fire to notice that the battle was over almost as quickly as it had begun.

As for Dec, his heart was pounding in his throat and his knees had turned to jelly. He was suddenly unable to stand and sagged slowly down to the deck. He had just enough presence of mind left to stuff the bit of resin into his pocket before he passed out.

Chapter 6

A JOURNEY SOUTH

LAELESTEQUENSTRUTIA SAT DOWN IN A PATCH OF GRASS BENEATH her tree and sighed. She had been very busy these last three days, paying old debts, returning things borrowed, saying goodbye to her many friends in the forest. She was beginning to feel as though she would never return, what with all the fuss and bother that had been made on her account . . . all the teary-eyed farewells, especially with dear old Myrna, who was like a mother to her. And then there was the matter of all the parting presents. She was only going to Castle Elfwood, for heaven's sake, not across the seas and over the edge of the world.

Laela was sorting these gifts out now, putting the ones she could use, like this bundle of burr root, very useful in making oneself invisible, into one pile. Those she did not need she placed in another pile. As she finished she surveyed the sorted-out gifts and pouted. The useful mound was much too large to fit into her travelling bag. Laela preferred to travel light, and as it was, she was burdened with all those scrolls given her by the elders, and the fancy clothes Myrna insisted she would have to wear in polite company, not to mention a disgusting pair of horribly uncomfortable leather shoes, which she thoroughly despised.

Sadly, she set aside the bags of nuts and berries. She could live without them. She ate the two apples, discarded two mistletoe wreaths and some bracelets, then tied the ends of the colorful gossamer scarfs to her belt. She twirled on tiptoe and noted with satisfaction the blur of color that swirled round her hips.

Sighing, she looked round and tried to think of something else, anything else that needed to be done, something that would defer the unpleasant moment of leavetaking. Unfortunately, she couldn't think of a thing. Even the dishes, her least favorite task, were washed and dried—polished to a sheen actually—and hung from the appropriate twigs. There was nothing left to do but leave. Lewtt twittered in her ear and settled on her shoulder, clinging tightly to one of her red curls. "I know, Lewtt," she said. "It's time to go." Laela took one last look around, and filling her eyes and her memory with all the infinite shades of green, the intricately twined branches, the song of the wind as it soughed through the treetops, she said farewell to her home.

Her heart was heavy as she made her way along the footpath that would eventually lead her out of the forest. She would gladly have changed into a falcon again, but she was burdened with bags of clothing . . . and all those scrolls. She would have to walk for a while, and perhaps summon one of her unicorn friends later. She found that she could not bear to look behind for a final glance at her home, fearing that the tears would start and never stop. Would she never see this place again? She knew what the old fusspot in the council had said, that this was a position of honor, an important mission, blah, blah, blah, but all the same, it felt like banishment, the worst of any possible punishment for her.

Her thoughts turned to Jaeme as she plodded resentfully along the forest trail under a hot sun that burned down unpleasantly on her shoulders. Jaeme had been a twit then; she was certain that he was a twit still. Somehow, during the course of the long, hot afternoon, all of her resentment, anger, and fears settled on Jaeme, as she had no one else to blame for her situation other than herself.

Three times that afternoon she whistled for a unicorn, but none appeared. Lewtt went off to search for one but returned empty-handed. Apparently all the mystical beasts were away to the north. To further darken her spirits, low grey clouds came rolling overhead and it began to look and smell like rain.

By the time she made her camp that evening, she was confused as to just who had become the root of all her problems, the elders, or Jaeme. She finally settled on old Fusspot and his companions as the unsuspecting repositories of all her rage, with Jaeme a close second.

Laela had settled into a fitful sleep when a sudden shower poured down on the forest after a single, sudden crack of thunder. Her mood was not improved by the thorough drenching she received. To make matters worse, all of her firewood was soaked, as well as her clothing, and she was unable to produce anything more than a pitiful, smoky fire that did nothing to drive out the chill. When morning finally dawned, a pearly, opalescent, glorious day, she was shivering and sniffling, her eyes felt scratchy, and her nose was red and drippy. Lewtt, who was never ill, was totally unsympathetic. He persisted in flitting about her head in a most annoying manner, saying all sorts of cheery things which only served to make her feel even more dreadful.

The young Druidess munched on a few nuts, then struggled, damp and unrested, to her feet. Unwillingly, she plodded on along the path, barely lifting her head to take her bearings. A breeze had sprung up, which at any other time would have been quite pleasant but now only chilled her further and whipped her hair into a nest of tangled knots. Her mood could not have been blacker when Lewtt, who had been flying on ahead to stay away from her black temper, suddenly spoke to her from afar, interrupting her thoughts.

Oh sadness, mistress, there has been a terrible fire and many trees are destroyed. The sprite did not elaborate and left her wondering, until he appeared before her and began hovering in front of her nose, twittering in the high-pitched voice he used when excited. To her fevered ears, it sounded like the shrill of a swarm of mosquitoes. She batted at the sprite, knowing that he was too swift for her.

"Top flitting awound, hode 'till and talk," she commanded irritably.

Lewtt did not even bother to laugh at her cold-snuffled words, which got her attention immediately. Lewtt would never pass up the opportunity to tease her.

The sprite landed on her shoulder, swept aside a mass of damp hair, and spoke directly into her ear.

Listen to me, mistress. There is danger ahead, the sprite said slowly and distinctly, making certain she got the message. *I have spied out those who set that fire. 'Tis a company of mounted men, armed as though for war. They are accompanied by a large number of footmen, also armed. You must take cover, for they are heading in this direction.*

Sudden fear lanced through Laela. She looked about her but, as luck would have it, the trail at this point led through one of the grassy leas that dotted the forest; there was nothing to be seen but a gently rolling grass-covered expanse. Her only hope was to hurry across the exposed clearing and take shelter in the forest; no one was her equal in the forest. Lewtt raised his arm and pointed. Laela followed the sprite's finger and saw a line of dark figures emerge from the edge of the forest before her, which was much closer than the forest behind. There was no way that they could avoid seeing her: she stood out like the proverbial bug on a toadstool. Even as she gnawed her lip, wondering what to do, a thready cry went up. She had been sighted!

She turned to run, but there was really nowhere to run to, and if they were mounted as the sprite had said, she could not hope to escape them. She thought about turning herself into a falcon and simply flying away, but then they would acquire her possessions, and little though they were, they were hers, and the mere idea of strangers pawing through her belongings made her angry. The more she thought about it, the angrier she got. Why should she run away and hide? She wasn't doing anything wrong! It was her forest. Let them go somewhere else!

All of her anger at being sent away from her beloved Elfwood, her fury at the dimly remembered Jaeme and her so-called assignment to the castle, not to mention the miserable night and the resulting nose cold, suddenly found an outlet. So they thought to have her on the run, did they! Laela began to fume. She placed her fists on her hips and glared at the rapidly advancing platoon, her foot tapping the ground, which for her was always a dead giveaway of furious thought. Lewtt, realizing what was about to happen, placed his hands over his eyes and groaned.

By the time the mounted men crested the final hill, Laela was ready for them. Lewtt had done his best to convince her to leave, had even yanked hard on a fistful of curls and got nothing but a swat for his troubles. Now, he fluttered above her left shoulder, biting his lip, hoping, nay, praying, that his mistress knew what she was doing.

There were twenty-four of them, mounted on horseback, and many more following behind on foot, all dressed in black tunics emblazoned with a yellow diamond. Their features were as dark and unforgiving as their garb. Any thoughts that Laela might have entertained about their being hapless travelers who had lost their way vanished at sight of their grim visages and weapons held at the ready as they advanced on a seemingly helpless female. Her last compunction disappeared as she dived into her duffel and tossed possessions out helter-skelter searching for the single item that might aid her.

Her hands closed upon the small cloth sack, her sensitive fingers knowing instantly that she had found it. She pulled it from the duffel and jerked open the mouth of the sack. No time for niceties—a glance told her that they would be on her in seconds. Ideally, the burr root should be ground to a powder, mixed with liquid, and heated till it bubbled, but it would work in its crude form as well, although not as well or for as long. At least it had gotten wet during last night's rainstorm. In one motion she pulled off her dress, then began rubbing the rough-barked root over her body, reciting the incantation, grateful for once that old Myrna had forced her to stay after class until she could recite the words backward as well as forward. When applied in the usual manner, the burr root caused one to disappear in a sudden poof, but since Laela was merely rubbing it on, she began to fade as the root passed over her skin.

The ground was shaking beneath the thunder of the war horses' hooves, so close to Laela now that a greenish-white rope of slathery foam flew from the lead horse's mouth onto her wrist just as the last bit of her faded from sight. Invisible, she stepped nimbly from the path, allowing the huge, hot beast to trample past.

The halberd swished past her head, uncomfortably close, too close actually. One could be killed, even if one was invisible! She turned in time to catch the look of astonishment that crossed the pikeman's face as she faded from sight, the blow with which he had clearly intended to kill her sliding harmlessly through the air. It was comical. Or would have been had the monstrous sweating horse not trampled on her bag of possessions and ground them into shreds beneath his enormous hooves. Any hopes she might have had to rescuing what remained were dashed by the following horses who pounded the small duffel into oblivion.

If she had had any doubts, they vanished in the swish of the pike and the shreds of her possessions. Who were these men and why were they in HER forest? Arms were an abomination, an insult to the ancient groves whose very existence, whose longevity, was a testament to peace and tranquillity. Fury filled her mind, and without a second thought, she uttered the words that launched her airborne. She became a whirlwind of feverish activity, using her invisible weight to swing a halberd sideways directly into the face of the following rider, knocking him senseless to the ground. Savoring the shouts of confusion and dismay, she slipped among the perplexed riders as they galloped past, and grabbed a foot, pushing it backward out of the stirrup, and then heaved up. The startled horseman gave a most satisfying yelp as he went crashing to the ground.

Growing bold with success, she darted among them, using their own weapons against themselves and each other. Soon, they forgot that they had ever seen her, for indeed, only the lead riders had done so and they were the first to fall. The remaining riders and armed footmen were left with no other thought than that their comrades had suddenly gone mad and begun attacking them. With blades whirling all about them, and no time for conversation, they could do nothing but fight back. Within a short period of time the once peaceful glen was a snarling mass of soldiers fighting to the death against those who only moments before had been their boon companions.

Laela stepped back to admire her handiwork. A job well done if she did say so herself. Lewtt hovered above her shoulder and chuckled gleefully.

That was very well done, my mistress! he exclaimed. *But do not tarry to admire your handiwork.* He fluttered down and landed on her wrist. *Your magic is beginning to fail*, he said, pointing at a patch of white skin, apparently floating in space.

She would have liked to stay and watch. It was most instructive and she was learning words she had never heard before, used in strange and unusual ways. But Lewtt was right; the burr root was beginning to wear off. She could see the edges of her body growing visible. The soldiers were still quite busy fighting among themselves, but Laela suspected that it would take little to change the focus of their hostilities.

The young Druidess turned on her heel and ran as quietly as possible over the grasses and into the safety of the forest, out of sight of the brawling, cursing mass of men. But even here it was not truly safe. If any one of them regained his senses and remembered the girl, he might calm his companions, and then they would undoubtedly come looking for her with a vengeance. Best to be gone from here as quickly as possible.

She could walk, but they could easily overtake her. She could fly on, but then she wouldn't have any clothes waiting for her when she landed. Somehow she doubted that the inhabitants of Elfwood Castle were ready to receive their new ambassadress *au-naturel*. Hoping against hope that some of her clothing had survived, she stayed on, hiding in the bushes, as the battle in the clearing wound to a bloody conclusion.

The mysterious force had proved deadly to the black-clad soldiers. When it finally came to an end, only seven nervous and shaken men remained. These few gathered what horses they could and rode quickly off, leaving their dead companions scattered about the field where they had fallen.

Lewtt flew out for a closer look, and followed the men for some distance.

'Tis safe, mistress, you may come forth, came his tiny voice from afar. Laela ventured cautiously into the field, giving each fallen man a wide berth. The grass was trampled and dark with blood. It got all over her feet and she became a bit queasy. At length she reached the point where her bag had been trampled. She shook her head sadly. The scrolls were destroyed beyond recognition. So were her leather shoes, provisions, and spare clothes. Miraculously, however, her dress and the scarves lay several feet to one side, muddy but otherwise unharmed. Her gold was still where she had hidden it.

The sprite arrived and began tugging at her hair mischievously. *Guess what? Guess what, mistress?* said Lewtt, buzzing excitedly in a circle around her head.

"What now?" she snapped as she pulled her one remaining garment back over her head.

Well, maybe I just won't tell you, Miss Snip Snap! She

swatted at him and missed, in no mood for his tricks and japes.

"I've just lost everything and you play jokes on me!" She chased him back to the edge of the wood.

Lewtt sensed her despair, landed on a tree branch out of reach, and spoke calmly. *'Tis a unicorn. You may ride now to Elfwood*!

"Hmmmm." Her face brightened, and rising to her feet, she placed two fingers in her mouth and let loose a most unladylike whistle, shrill and penetrating, which flew through the forest like an arrow. Shortly thereafter, she was rewarded by the sound of hoofbeats, delicate and dainty hoofbeats, unlike the thunderous stomping of the massive war horses. A lovely, soft whickering filled the air, and warm, fragrant breath drifted across Laela's shoulder. Turning, she beheld a most wondrous sight.

It was an old unicorn, yet still slim and graceful as a moonbeam, dancing on impossibly tiny hoofs that shone with crystalline brilliance, deflecting rays of light with its every movement.

It was, of course, purest white, although white was a totally inadequate description, just as yellow cannot describe the splendor of the sun, or the word blue describe the glory of the sky. To look upon the magical creature was like looking upon the pearly opalescence of mist as it drifts across a moonlit glade, or the shimmering of silvery stars strewn across a black velvet summer sky. It was beauty personified, its passage more graceful than the flutter of a butterfly's wing. To ride upon a unicorn was to ride the wind, to sail among the clouds. And it would obey her every command; its allegiance was hers for the taking.

Unfortunately, Lewtt, being male, did not enjoy the same privileges, since unicorns shunned the presence of men, even male sprites. Smiling smugly, Laela leaped upon the unicorn's back and clung to its silky mane as it reared high on its hind legs and plunged instantly into the forest. Threading its way among the trees almost faster than the eye could see, the unicorn left Lewtt to trail behind disconsolately, following as best he could.

Almost immediately, they began to encounter a thick black smoke which burned the eyes and stung the nostrils. Homeless animals streamed past them—deer, rabbit, lynx, squirrels—leaping from tree to tree. Many of them bore unmistakable signs of fire, charred bits of fur and flesh, but even more ominous was the sadness in their eyes which stabbed at Laela like the thrust of a knife. She spurred the unicorn forward, although it was obviously reluctant to go any further. Eyes grim, she insisted.

Seated astride the unicorn's back as it wound slowly through the scene of desolation, Laela looked out onto a blackness such as she had never seen in all her young life. Everywhere she looked the forest had been burned; all was black and still smoking. Some of the trees, their enormous trunks wider around than four men could reach, older than the oldest of the Druids elders, were destroyed, their branches now broken and charred, hanging useless at their sides.

It was fortunate indeed, Laela thought, that there had been a downpour just the night before or the damage would have been far worse. She now blessed the rain that had soaked her. Even so, the dead trees made her sad, and those who were wounded and barely alive called to her in their quiet tree voices as though in agony.

Laela clapped her hands over her ears, unable to bear the horrible sounds. She felt as though she herself was dying.

She tried to rationalize the anguished cries, telling herself that the sounds were caused by nothing more than the remaining heat consuming the trees' sap, that the trees were not really feeling pain, that they were not dead or dying. But logical explanations had little power against the horror she was experiencing. She was a Druid. Her whole life, her whole reason for living, her very soul, was intrinsically entwined with the forest. The forest WAS her soul.

She looked out at the dead trees and felt as though a part of herself was dead as well. She was heartsick, wounded at the core, injured more severely than by any pikestaff or sword. She looked on helpless and hopeless, unable to do anything to help her beloved forest.

She knew there were balms and unguents which the elders used to save the dying, but such knowledge had not yet been imparted to her. Laela reached up and grasped Lewtt. The sprite had fallen silent too.

"Fly now to Myrna and take her this ill news," she told Lewtt. "Let her tell the elders to bring help and new seed." The sprite was off without a word. Laela's heart hardened irrevocably against the men dressed in black emblazoned with the yellow diamond. She did not know whose flag they followed, to whom they knelt in obeisance, but she would find out. And as the tears coursed down her cheeks, she vowed that they would pay and perish in agony as had her beloved forest.

At last Laela and the unicorn rode out of the burned forest and were back among the living. The remainder of the journey, however, was accomplished in silence. There was nothing to say. Lewtt, when he returned, attempted to relieve the heavy quietude several times, but a single, piercing thought and glance from Laela was all that it took to silence him. Never had she looked at him like that. It was as if she had suddenly become a grownup!

Lewtt hovered far above his mistress, well out of sight, and shivered at the thought. Laela a grownup. He could not believe, did not want to believe, that his fun-loving, mischievous companion was gone forever. Why, if the truth be told, which Lewtt went to great extremes to avoid, Laela was far better than he at thinking up mischief! Some of their very best pranks had been her ideas. Like the time they had spread fast-drying glue on the seats of the high council and all the old greybeards had stuck fast in their robes. Had to strip out of their clothes—ohh, would he ever forget the sight of all those skinny, pale white, hairy old shanks! Ughhh!—and slip into new robes before they could even begin to think of who had done such an irreverent thing. They never found out.

Laela had planted the glue pot and the brush under the bed of a jealous rival, Kraftequennia. It had been Krafty who had reported to the council that Laela colored her hair with thickwhistel berries. Krafty was eventually exonerated, for they could not prove that she had done it, but she had been much subdued, which pleased Laela immensely. Lewtt was still fretting over Laela's unusual decorum when the unicorn left the woods behind and trotted to a halt atop a grassy swale. Before them the grass sloped gently down to the banks of the River Tyrell. Across the river, situated on a bluff, stood Castle Elfwood.

"You can come down now, Lewtt. We have arrived," Laela announced. A much relieved sprite fluttered down from the sky and landed in his mistress's red hair.

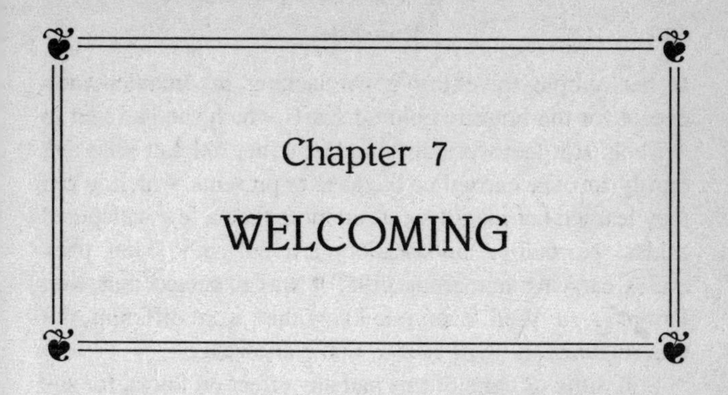

Chapter 7
WELCOMING

NOT EVEN LAELA COULD FAULT HER RECEPTION AT ELFWOOD CASTLE. No sooner had she been spied atop the hill than a crowd began to gather. At first, they had been guardsmen, armed to the teeth, a fact which was clear even at that distance. Then, a mirror flashed in the sunlight and a cry went up. The castle gates opened wide and throngs of people poured out across the lowered bridge, hurrying forward to greet her.

The unicorn had no liking for crowds, even those without large numbers of men, and it shied and danced on its hind legs, almost unseating Laela. Its discomfort was obvious, and as much as Laela longed to turn around and gallop back into the forest, she was bound by her duty and her promise more securely than by any lock and chain. She sighed deeply, stroked the unicorn's soft neck, and slid down from its back. No sooner had her feet touched the ground than the unicorn wheeled and darted back over the bridge, up the swale, and into the forest, vanishing like a raindrop in drought. She watched it until the spot it had entered began to blur. Then she turned to meet the rapidly advancing crowd. There were a few odd glances and raised eyebrows at her simple travelling gown lacking in ornamentation except for the brightly colored scarfs which she had tied to her belt. Her feet were dirty and bare, her red hair wild and unruly, and she carried no baggage or presents, which, when they learned her identity, caused more than a few whispered asides. Normally, ambassadors arrived with laden pack mules carrying numerous gifts. It was expected, but with Druids . . . Well, everyone knew they were different, not like regular folk. One had to make allowances.

Still, little or none of this had any effect on Laela, for she was totally unaccustomed to the ways of regular humanfolk. In the manner of all Druids, Laela was frank and open. Thus, the insincere comments and compliments paid to her by the women of the court were accepted at face value and their givers thanked prettily, which only served to make them feel small and very uncomfortable.

She had been escorted inside the gates and greeted in the main courtyard by an old greybeard dressed in rich robes hung with heavy chains of gold. He introduced himself as one Polonius. He was pleasant enough and welcomed her most genuinely, although she couldn't help noticing that he seemed somewhat distracted and his features were strained with signs of recent grief.

She noticed more than one pair of reddened eyes as she passed through the immense and impressive castle, following the elderly man and a giggling chorus of handmaidens through a bewildering maze of stone-flagged halls.

At last they arrived at the chambers which were to be hers. They were located deep within the heart of the castle, and even though the rooms themselves were quite nice—the floors covered with thick rugs, the dark walls and furniture hung with tapestries, the ceilings so high as to be lost in gloom—Laela's heart sank. She felt as though she were buried beneath an immense weight, in danger of being crushed by the pressure of the castle walls. She hung back, pressed against the door, pale and shaken.

"What's the matter, my dear? Is the room not to your liking?" Polonius may have been an old greybeard, the likes of whom she was more in the habit of teasing than trusting, but he had not risen to his position of prominence by right of his family name. The young woman's distress was obvious. She could do no more than nod.

Amid a chorus of disbelief from the women gathered round—"Why, it's the nicest room in the castle, no breezes to chill you or windows to let in the cold!"—Polonius was suddenly aware of the situation and smartly dismissed the gaggle of women with a single curt gesture.

"I know just the place for you, m'dear!" Polonius took Laela by the hand and led her through ever narrowing corridors, descending until they emerged just short of the kitchen. The air was redolent with the warm, yeasty scent of fresh bread, meat browning over the hearth, and a plethora of fresh herbs.

Throwing open a small door, Polonius entered a room, which though spacious according to what Laela had known, was quite small by gentry standards. Upon its rush-strewn floors there was only a single bed covered with clean homespun linen, a plain wood table and a straight back, plank-bottomed chair. Its single, gracious feature were two large windows that opened directly upon the kitchen gardens, an extensive and highly productive bit of land tucked against an outer wall. There were numerous fruit trees, one of which, a golden apple, brushed up against the window shutters. The room was filled with an abundance of sunlight, and although it would be hot in the summer and cold in the winter, Laela thought it perfect. Despite the fact that he was probably an old fusspot greybeard, Laela flung herself upon Polonius, wrapped her arms around his neck, and squeezed him tight. Her eyes were shining.

"Thank you," she whispered. Then she leaped through the window, skirts flying around her delicate ankles as she slipped between tall, ripening rows of corn and disappeared from sight. Her exuberant joyous shout trailed back, startling a crow who took flight from his perch on a scarecrow.

Polonius cleared his throat judiciously and smoothed his beard and mustache to cover the grin that threatened to spread across his face. "Ahemm, rumff, hrmph, yes, of course, quite all right. Quite all right," he said to himself as he retraced his steps back to the main hall. Quite an odd choice for an ambassadress, he thought, quite odd, even for the Druids, but somehow he was sure they would get on quite well indeed. Those eyes, he mused wonderingly, unaware that his old legs were skipping lightly up a flight of stairs . . . Had he ever seen eyes quite so green before?

When Dec awakened, he blinked, unable to comprehend what it was that he was seeing. He was lying on the hard, too-short board that was his shipboard bunk—he could tell that immediately from the ache in his protesting muscles and the manner in which his head drooped, unsupported, below his body. And he was still aboard ship—that was clear from the rise and fall of his bunk and the piercing cry of the gulls. But instead of peering upward at grimy dark boards a mere ten inches from his nose, he was looking directly out upon a blue, cloud-filled sky! The roof to his cabin appeared to have vanished completely! Even as he pondered the phenomenon, heavy footsteps clattered nearby, the door to his cabin—now a most unnecessary fixture—was thrown open, and he was set upon by numerous hands.

To his amazement, he found himself lifted on high, hoisted to the shoulders of the crew, and carried out on deck. By twisting his head, he was able to see that the ship had sustained terrible damage. Some great force had destroyed almost all of the afterdeck. The lower cabins, his included, were all that remained, and their upper walls ended in ragged, still smoking, charred timbers.

His head was aching horribly. Had he been injured? He pressed a hand to his throbbing temples and then, in a flash, it came back to him. He! He, Decutonius Consulus, was the source of the damage. He had gotten the spell wrong and had blown his own ship apart! Oh, he had really done it this time. He groaned, grateful for only one thing, that he would not live to face his father's disappointment. He had no doubt that the sailors, having extinguished the fire he had caused, were now about to fling him overboard, a fate which he certainly deserved.

Much to his astonishment, he was plunked down on a newly polished deck and steadied by careful hands. He found himself facing the captain and the full complement of sailors. Many of them bore evidence of the fire, eyebrows frizzled, beards and hair stinking with smoke, burns on hands and clothes. He gulped. "I can explain," he said in a small voice.

The captain clapped him on the back, and once more he found himself hoisted high, this time upon the captain's own broad shoulders.

"Three cheers for the wizard!" bellowed Bottinius in a deep baritone. "Huzzah! Huzzah! Huzzah!" roared the men.

"Never seen such a thing in all my days," said the

captain, a broad grin covering his face as he finally lowered Dec. "Ye blew them Northmen all to smithereens!"

"I did?" Dec stammered. "Uh, uh, I mean, well, I, uh, there was nothing else for it. Yes, yes, I had to do it," he said, the memory finally returning. "But, what have I done to your beautiful ship?"

"Well, yes, there's that." Bottinius rubbed his hand over his grizzled chin, surveyed the damage aft, and then brought his face close to Dec's. The smell of his rum-flavored breath was as potent a weapon as Dec had ever known. Obviously the captain had already begun the celebration.

"To tell ye the truth," he whispered, the fumes giving Dec a heady rush. "I never liked the design all that much, the ol' *Gosser* were a wee bit top heavy . . . she wallowed like a duck in heavy seas, and were loath t'answer the helm. Ye done me a favor if the truth be known!" He lifted a thick, calloused finger to his lips and blew, signaling a secret, and then he winked. Dec winked back, not sure he quite knew what the man was talking about and stunned at his good fortune.

For the remainder of the day he was toasted, by every sailor on board, and had downed more than a few toasts himself so as not to appear rude. The commotion was so exhilarating that he could hardly comprehend it. He was not accustomed to being congratulated on the outcome of his experiments. Perhaps for the first time in his life he had done something right. Something big and important. He thought he could learn to like it, and by evening he was accepting praise and compliments as though they were the norm.

Rising the next morn was a far more unpleasant chore. He raised a hand to his aching head, which felt several sizes too large, and did his best to block out the bright sun that shone down upon him unobstructed by the deck above. The roof of his mouth tasted like the bottom of a tar bucket, and he groaned, vowing never, never again in his entire life to lift another glass of grog. How could something that tasted so good make him feel so bad? The young mage toyed with the idea of using one of his own spells, a curative, to make himself feel better. But it hurt too much even to think, and nothing which did come to mind seemed appropriate. He could shrink his head, literally, but what was the good of that? And if by some chance he couldn't reverse it, he had no desire to go through life with a shrunken head.

By the time they were approaching port, late in the afternoon, Dec was feeling much improved—until the cook offered him a plate of salt pork with pease porridge. Dec flew to the to the rail, shaken with dry heaves.

The damaged *Goshawk* limped into a sheltered harbour, surrounded on three sides by low, tree-covered hills. There was a long, timbered pier that extended out into the bay, and several smaller boats were tied up to it. Many locals gathered to watch as the wounded ship finally tied up.

The local authorities were shocked to hear that the *Goshawk* had been attacked by Northmen, and a cheer went up among the crowd on shore when the captain expounded upon the deeds of the new mage of Elfwood. Dec smiled from the rail and waved at the crowd, quite pleased with himself.

His baggage was brought on deck by the crew and Dec stood by the gangway ready to leave.

"I've taken the liberty of hiring ye a coach that'll take ye straight away t' the Castle Elfwood." Bottinius looked apologetic. "We're a day late and many leagues south of where we should have landed. All the same, it be no mor'n a two-day trip if ye rides hard."

Dec shook the captain's hand one last time, waved his farewells to the crew, and staggered down the plank to the pier. The two crewmen with his bag pushed the crowd aside and he followed them down to a cobbled street where a small closed coach was drawn up awaiting his arrival.

The sailors piled his baggage in the back and helped Dec climb inside. They thanked him again and then disappeared among the crowd. The coach and its driver, a small, dour, untalkative fellow, set off with a jerk. Dec had hoped to spend the night in an inn, sleeping and coddling his aching head, but it seemed the driver had other plans.

Even though it was his first official hangover, Dec was young, healthy, and strong, and the blasts of fresh air surging in through the open windows, coupled with his joy at being off the sea and travelling through a new and foreign land, soon restored his natural sense of enthusiasm. He peered out the windows, anxious to get a glimpse of this strange new world. Unfortunately, as he soon discovered to his acute disappointment, it bore a striking resemblance to the countryside surrounding Lundinum.

They were travelling down a narrow lane through the outskirts of the port town whose name he had failed to catch. The houses were built higgledy-piggledy, stacked one next to the other, crowded densely together, just like those at home, each with a small garden in front. The coach made a sharp turn, and now they were passing out into the countryside, where there were stables and barnyards, and sheep could be seen grazing in pastures. Many carts clattered by laden with fresh produce, and the coach came to a sudden stop as a shepherd guided his flock around them, heading, no doubt, toward a central market.

They rode on, through a small wood that quickly opened out into pastureland, past farms and occasionally a small castle. Small towns appeared and disappeared, flashing past Dec's window as the coach pounded along steadily without hesitation. His throat grew dry, his stomach was empty and his bladder full, yet the coach showed no sign of stopping. His headache had returned with a vengeance and night was crowding in on all sides when finally he perceived a slowing of the coach's pace. He stuck his head outside the window, expecting to see a town or, at the very least, a roadside inn, but there was nothing in sight except the road, some distant hills, and a small grove of trees.

The driver carefully edged the coach off onto the embankment and then leaped down from his high seat to lead the snorting team of horses down to the grove of trees. Here, he unhitched them from their traces and began to wipe them down with a coarse cloth, patting their steaming flanks and flicking the foam from their lathered necks. He murmured to them in a soft, comforting tone. When he finally finished his ministrations, he allowed them to drink a small amount of water from the tiny stream that wound its way through the trees, then let them graze upon the grasses that grew nearby.

Dec, who had meanwhile been relieving himself among the trees, cleared his throat as though to speak. The driver paid him no heed. Dec cleared his throat a little louder. "Ahem, AHEM!" At last, the little man turned to look at him.

"Uh, are we going to spend the night here?" Dec asked politely. The man merely nodded and returned to his tasks. Dec sighed. Nothing was ever simple. He walked upstream, above the horses, and knelt down for a drink. He had no food and no supplies to make himself comfortable, but he could build a fire and at least be warm. He wandered around the small stand of trees until he had gathered up a sufficient amount of wood. Then he returned to an opening he had noted, a small glen in the center of the wood, and here he arranged his pile of sticks. A few carefully spoken words and the sticks burst into flames, throwing a warm, cheery glow across the small area, as well as taking the edge off the evening chill. Dec seated himself before the flames and tried to ignore the grumbling of his belly.

To his surprise, the coachman joined him after a time, tossing him a coarse, heavy blanket that smelled of horse sweat. Dec was too surprised to do more than mumble his thanks. The coachman grunted and seated himself before the fire, whereupon he handed Dec a small round of cheese, half an onion, and the heel from a loaf of black bread. Dec was too hungry to complain about the meagerness of the fare and downed it to the last scrap.

He tried to make conversation, but the driver was clearily uninterested in anything he had to say. In mid-sentence, the man wrapped himself in his blanket, turned his back on Dec, and was snoring almost before his head touched the ground.

''Well, a very good night to you, Mr. Nameless,'' Dec muttered, wondering if everyone in these northern lands would be as surly. He tried to remember what he had heard of Elfwood, but it was a subject about which he knew little, and nothing sprang to mind. His father had told him that Castle Elfwood was located on the edge of the oldest part of the ancient forest, and that the forest was a precious and wonderful place, inhabited by magic creatures and a race of Druids who kept mostly to themselves, but he didn't know anything else. He racked his brain, scouring it for tiny bits of elusive memory.

Druids. Well, yes. Again, everyone knew that the Druids lived in Elfwood along with sprites and elves and fairies, although many people of recent years had begun saying that there were no such things, that they were only the stuff of bedtime stories. Such folk considered themselves modern and scoffed at anyone who still believed.

Yet Dec still believed, and he had good cause to. Those same folk who proclaimed elves and fairies and sprites to be nonsense also proclaimed magic to be trickery and sleight of hand. There was an ominous tendency among people who considered themselves "upper class" to dismiss the art he practiced as well as all the other elements of Dweomercraft. It was frightening. If such a trend were to gain strength, why, anything could happen. People might even stop believing in magic and wizards completely! It was a frightening thought. For a moment he wondered, would magic stop working if people stopped believing in it? Then he laughed, rose to his feet, and wrapped the horse blanket around himself. Why bother thinking of things that would never come to be? A world without magic was unimaginable. Still smiling at his own dark thoughts, Dec settled himself on the ground and fell instantly asleep.

They were on the move before daybreak, rattling across a countryside that became ever more bleak and isolated as the miles rolled past. Dec could hardly believe that people still lived in such a place. The road had changed to a pair of dusty, bumpy ruts, and the towns, further and further apart now, were no more than a gathering of huts surrounding a large fortified home or keep, with perhaps an inn and a smith.

They stopped at one such place at midday to change the horses. Dec descended from the coach to relieve himself and instantly found himself the center of watchful attention. The eyes were not friendly. He attempted to speak to one or two of the men, but they merely grunted and turned away from him. He thought to speak to one of the women—until he noticed that every man was armed and none of the women were unescorted.

''Here, lad. You'll be needin' this.'' The coachman thrust a bulging cloth sack into Dec's hands, then stood beside the coach, holding the door open. The message was clear. The young mage took his seat on the hard bench, and once more they were off, leaving the town behind them in a cloud of dust.

The sack, much to Dec's pleasure, contained two small roasted hens, more cheese, several apples, and a small loaf of bread. All of which he consumed, down to the last crumb, by the time the windows of the coach were black with night. They stopped again. Dec looked out dispiritedly, expecting yet another tiny town or small wood, but instead, he saw the outline of a magnificent castle, sitting atop a low hill, silhouetted against moonlit clouds. Fires burned all along the ramparts, and he could see the figures of men, their helmets and chain mail gleaming in the moonlight, pacing the high walls, armed with pikes and spears. Other fires burned as well, illuminating the towers at every corner and the mullioned windows, some with glass catching the light and flinging it back. He noticed that most of the small windows were barred. A river flowed between them and the castle. There was a heavy iron portcullus in front of the double gates that led into the fortification, its joints reinforced by heavy welds. As Dec watched, the barrier was drawn up with a ratchety screeching of metal, the double gates were pulled aside, and a drawbridge inched its way down until it landed on the far side with a heavy thunk. The coach rattled across the slender wood bridge. Observing the armed men with suspicious eyes standing to either side, Dec clutched the edge of the seat and wondered what on earth he had gotten himself into.

The coach drew to a halt in the lower bailey. Instantly, the door was thrown open and a circle of men-at-arms, their hands on the hilts of their weapons, stood waiting for him to descend.

Dec was not a coward, but he had never before experienced anything like the situation confronting him. It was, well, it was almost as though these people were at war and were thinking that he might be the enemy!

He thought back to his last day at school. Reginal Portinbras, the son of a rich man, a lad with no talent whatsoever, who had always been jealous of him, had appeared to shake his hand and bid him farewell. Dec had thought it odd at the time, but Reginal had laughed and asked him why he thought he was being sent to Elfwood. Dec had replied that Elfwood had petitioned the council for a wizard and they had granted the request. Reginal had all but fallen down laughing. Elfwood he informed Dec, had petitioned the council for the past six years and had never been granted a wizard. Elfwood was deemed too dangerous for wizards, who were in short supply as it was. That is, until Dec had been so good as to blow up the school. Then, the head Wizard and his council had suddenly decided that Elfwood's request should indeed be granted. Reginal had shown his true colors then, looking down disdainfully at Dec and curling his lip in a sneer. The council, he informed Dec, would have thrown him out on his ear had his father not been too influential to offend. As it was, they were sending him to Elfwood, where, with any luck, he would soon be killed. "Farewell, toad." Reginal had left with another laugh.

Dec had shrugged the incident off as nothing more than jealousy, but looking out the window at the throng of grim faced men who were staring at him, it now seemed ominously real.

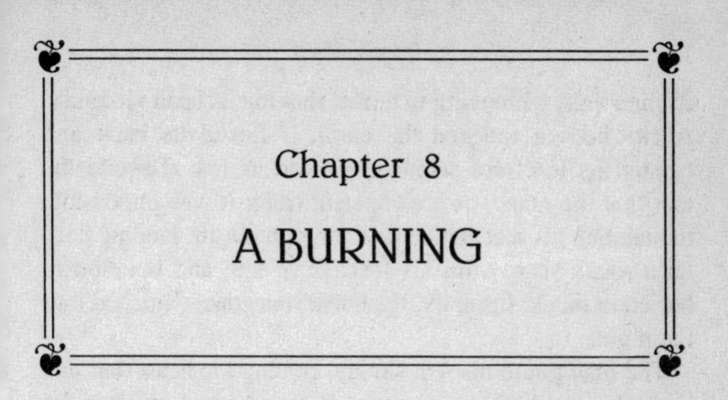

Chapter 8

A BURNING

THE NIGHT WAS DARK, SUITABLY DARK FOR THE SORT OF BUSINESS he was about, thought the rider to himself as he stared up at the inky sky. No moon, no stars to be seen, an eerie fog creeping across the moors. He drew the collar of his cloak tighter about his throat and shivered. The fog, as dense and white as a comber, hit him at the waist astride his horse. Afoot, it wrapped itself around his face and clung as though it wished to take him down and suck the breath from his lungs.

He tried to laugh at his own frightening imagery, but the sound twisted in his throat and came out a dry croak. A ghostly howl rose behind him and he clutched the hilt of his sword and turned in the saddle, even though he knew that there would be nothing to see. The howl was joined in mid-pitch by a second and then a third and . . . more! They were all around him. Ascending in volume and then sinking away, no two the same. The flesh on the back of his neck crawled at the horrid sound! His horse began to dance beneath him and he clung to the reins with both hands, trying to bring the beast under control. The animal rose on its hind legs, whinnying in terror, shaking its head violently. As its hooves touched the earth, it flexed its back and twisted its forefront sideways toward its rear. Despite the fact that the man was a competent rider, it was impossible to maintain his seat and he flew through the air, landing hard on a rocky scarp with his feet above him and his elbows buried in muck. Instantly, the horse was gone, vanished into the night.

The man got to his feet slowly, cursing the beast that had borne him and all its ancestors. Before he had reached the end of his colorful vocabulary, there was a terrible scream that ended abruptly. Then there was nothing to be heard but the crunching of bone and the rending of flesh.

The man inched slowly backward, searching for a place of safety—a rock, a tree, something, anything—to protect his back, even though he knew there was no such place in this flat and barren land. But the horse would not keep the wolves long, and then they would come looking for him.

A hand gripped his shoulder and he almost fell to the ground, his knees and bowels turned to water. Fear was a bitter, coppery taste in his mouth. He turned, struggling to raise his sword, to die like a man. He was met with jeering, raucous laughter.

"Scared yuh, huh!" More guffaws followed. The man was so relieved that it took him a while to turn his fear into anger. He straightened, stood tall, and raised his sword in a manner that caused the hideous, loathsome creatures gathered round him to still their laughter.

The foggy blackness now glowed orange by the light of several dim torches, held by a group of orcs. The Pictish Wastes were their place, their territory. He had come to them and they outnumbered him vastly. But still, he had his ways and they had tasted his anger and the bite of his sword before. They were cunning and devious and knew when it was best to cease and desist. The time would come when they had gained what they sought. Then . . . they would no longer fear the man or his sword.

Oldung, their leader—taller, broader of shoulder and stronger than any of the others—stepped forward. He and the man walked apart. The man did his best to shut out the sound of his noble stallion being consumed by ravenous teeth. Notwithstanding its moment of fear, it had been a fine and courageous beast. These miserable creatures would pay for its loss . . . when the time came.

The bargaining began. The man was sickened by the need to haggle with creatures as disgusting and lowly as orcs. It was beneath him, beneath everything he had been raised to revere. He chided himself silently, remembering what was at stake and the real need to deal with creatures such as these. He forced his face into a look of caring, as though he could care for scum like this, but his face revealed nothing but sincerity.

The orc leader pressed his advantage, demanding even more than had been agreed upon. The man cursed the foul being, and sought to remind it of the bargain struck weeks before, then realized the foolishness of such an action. Orcs had no honor, the concept was foreign to them. He knew that if he did not agree to the new demands, the orcs were likely to renege on the whole affair and he would lose all that he had invested.

He considered that option briefly, but it was impossible. He had come too far to turn back now; bridges had been burned that could never be rebuilt. He stifled his rage and nodded once, acquiescing to their demands, holding his face still, not allowing any portion of his rage to glimmer through. Fortunately, he had anticipated just such an occurence, and the mules were laden with the anticipated increase in booty. He knew, too, that the mules themselves would share the fate of his stallion, but that was the cost of doing business with orcs.

The word Harrowhall leaped out of the darkness, part of the rambling, near incoherent speech that the orc was spewing. The man seldom listened to its words—they were seldom worth listening to—but this was different. He turned on the orc in a fury that caused the loathsome creature to stumble backward in amazement.

"Never mention that word, or my name, or anything else about this business! Never!" the man hissed, his eyes narrow slits of obsidian. His body was trembling, not from fear, but like that of a sword stressed to the point of snapping. "All of our dealings are to be a complete secret. No one, not your men, not anyone, must know of this. DO . . . YOU . . . UNDERSTAND . . . ME!" Oldung nodded gravely, his eyes open wide, watching the man carefully in case he did lose control and go berserk. One could never be too careful with humans, they were so unpredictable.

The two of them, man and orc, walked back to the larger gathering of orcs, whereupon the leader passed along the information that their demands had been met. The exchange was in the orcish tongue, really no more than a piglike series of grunts, clicks, and snorts, thought the man, even though he was certain the words contained some sort of insult. He knew they were laughing at him. He could scarcely maintain his calm, and promised himself that every one of the brutish beings would die when he was done with them.

The man now led Oldung and three others through the fog, surrounded on all sides by lean gray ghostlike wraiths—the wolves, the orcs' boon companions. Now and then one ventured too close and received a calloused toe in the ribs or a club on the head for its troubles. Such rough treatment never seemed to affect them for long, for wolves and orcs intermingled like little boys and puppies.

He knew they were nearing the place where he had bid his men-at-arms to wait with the mules, by the shrill yapping of the wolves, the air of anticipation that came over them as they leaped and frolicked, no doubt anticipating the gristly feast to come. The orcs had increased the pace as well, and now the man could hear the terrified hee-hawing of the mules and the shouts of his men as they did their best to control the horses and the string of pack mules.

The smoky glare of torches stained the fog blood-red, doing little to relieve the press of darkness. He had forbidden his men to show a light, but their fear of the dark and the things it concealed had been greater than their fear of him. Normally, he would make them pay for such a transgression, for daring to disobey him, but he could understand, for he shared their terror.

The exchange was carried out in an instant, the men handing over the traces of the frightened mules, their eyes rolling white in the firelight, teeth bared in a helpless show of strength. The man averted his eyes as the pack animals were hauled from the camp, protesting every step of the way. They were dumb creatures, but even they knew what lay in store for them. The man's stomach turned. They were only mules, stupid beasts whose only purpose was to serve man, but even they were far superior to the orcs, surely the lowest, most disgusting form of life that existed.

His men crowded behind him, placing him squarely between themselves and the orcs, their swords drawn, jostling one another violently for the supposed safety of an inner position. As though anywhere would be safe if the orcs had taken it in their minds, their tiny minds, to attack.

And these were some of his bravest men. The man sneered at them, letting them see his scorn, then he turned back to the orcs and did his best to hide his own fear.

The orc leader paused a moment, waiting until the last of the mules was dragged away. Then he called out, "The little village at the edge of the wood, within the week, Felker!" repeating the place and the time they had agreed upon.

Felker hissed, raging inside, and waved Oldung away, knowing that the orc had uttered the forbidden words intentionally, both as an insult and a threat, letting him know that if the orcs so chose, there was nothing he could do to control them. He had purchased the use of their fearsome strength, and nothing more. As he watched them disappear into the darkness, the master of Harrowhall could not help but wonder who had forged the better deal.

Andrew the Smith, was standing at his well situated beneath an immense tree at the rear of his forge, admiring the sunset. Fierdras was but a little place, no more than a meeting of two little-travelled roads at the edge of the Elfwood, south of and too near the Pictish Wastes. Twenty leagues west and north of the Castle Elfwood, there was little reason for its existence. It stood near the remains of Offa's Wall, and there were some who said that once a great and important town had stood there, transacting commerce on both highways.

It may have been true—there was not a person alive in the village who could not bring forth some relic, a bit of worked metal, a shard of broken pottery with the old imperial design still visible, or even a knife, the metal brittle and pitted with age. The village may well have once been a site of importance, but now it was just a sleepy little hamlet, home to just over sixty souls, farmers for the most part, and they were the most distant folk to call the Lord of Elfwood their master. But the soil was stony and poor, and it was difficult to support a family on what they were able to grow. Andrew suspected that the town would cease to exist one day, perhaps sooner than later. Already, a number of the younger folk had left to seek their fortunes elsewhere. Andrew sighed. He would not like to leave Fierdras if it could be avoided. It was home, and in his opinion, it offered some of the finest sunsets he had ever seen, anywhere. The fact that he had never been anywhere else, save to the castle twice a year to shoe their horses, mattered little to his way of thinking.

He was still wrapped in the warmth of his enjoyment, leaning against the rough bark of the ancient bay tree, observing the wash of reds and pinks and yellows that filled the horizon, when he heard a sound that had no place in his current reveries. It was a hideous sound, a high-pitched, terror-filled scream. A woman in some sort of terrible distress!

Fierdras may not have been a great metropolis, they may not have enjoyed many of the luxuries of larger towns, but one thing they did enjoy was a freedom from fear. There was little to be fearful of, an occasional attack of a wild animal when in the woods, but certainly not in the center of town. Andrew could think of nothing that would cause a woman to scream like that. All of this raced through his head as he lumbered heavily back through the yard which also served as a holding pen for horses waiting to be shod. He grabbed up a hammer from the smoky, dark interior of his shop and then stared out at a shocking scene.

The front of the shop was built with low walls to allow the heat of the forge to disperse. During the summer, the space between wall and roof was left open; during the winter months, a wall built of willow lathes was fitted into the opening. This being high summer, the wall was down, providing a clear view of what was happening in the village square.

Despite himself, Andrew's jaw fell open and waves of terror washed over him. He gripped the edge of his workbench to keep from falling to his knees. More blood-curdling screams and cries of agony filled the air. His hand reached blindly for a better weapon, even as he realized the futility of such an action.

It was orcs. More orcs than he had ever seen in his life. Never had he seen more than one or two, and those always at a distance and at night. Now the loathsome monsters filled the small village, overrunning it like swarming pigs in the oak mast. They were everywhere, both in and out of houses, swinging terrible double-edged axes, killing everything and everyone. Men, women, children, horses, pigs, even dogs and cats, were being dragged out and hewn apart, their blood streaming down the lane in dusty rivulets. The attack had been so swift that there was no hope for a defense. The few men who had managed to reach their weapons, so seldom necessary in this quiet backwater, had been mercilessly hacked to pieces.

Andrew fought with himself. A part of him, the part that cherished his quiet home and his way of life, that valued the men, women, and children whom he had known all his life, wanted nothing more than to rush out into the square and do his best to slay as many of the hideous creatures as possible before he himself added his body to the growing numbers of the dead. Was there any life for him or reason to live if all he had known and loved was gone? But even as he argued with himself, took the first step forward that would lead him to his death, another voice spoke out inside his head. What if this was not an isolated incident? What if the orcs continued their rampage, spreading death and destruction to other unsuspecting villages? Better to live and warn others so that they might be prepared to defend themselves.

Even though the logic of this argument was impossible to ignore, Andrew had a hard time preventing himself from an immediate attempt to avenge friends and family. He stood there in the descending darkness, shaking and trembling like a wild horse, roped and captive, subservient for the first time to a will other than his own. It was not a good feeling.

A sound brought him back to the moment, instantly alert. The orcs were running amok in the houses and stores, throwing everything that caught their eye out into the open where it formed jumbled piles, mingling with the dead to whom the items had once belonged. Here was a polished box with a length of pink ribbon curled within, there a doll looking deceptively like a small infant. An orc sliced its head off. A chair tumbled out of a door and was flung upon the mounting pile. Andrew wondered how they would separate what they wanted, how they would know who . . . Wait, what were they doing! He stared in horror and disbelief, his eyes seeing but his mind refusing to comprehend.

They had not looted the buildings to gain possessions but to create a vast pyre! An orc ran out of a house carrying a straw torch, flaming in the tender darkness of early evening. He hurled it on the mixed pile of bodies and burnables and leaped up and down howling with glee. A soft gather of curtains ignited and shot up in a spire of flames.

Orc after orc followed his lead and soon every house in the village was aflame. Andrew could hear his own thatch roof crackling above him. It was a miracle that none had yet come into his shop. Acrid smoke filled his lungs, but still he could not leave, for it seemed that some of those lying upon the mound were not dead but were twisting in agony as the fires licked their limbs.

He wanted to rush to their rescue, to put them out of their misery with one swift blow, but the orcs had now formed a circle around the fire and were dancing and leaping and working themselves into a slavering frenzy. Andrew knew that he would never reach the fire alive. There was nothing he could do.

The fire bit into the thatch now. Taking great bites out of the thick dry straw, it snapped and snarled above him, and the first tiny tendrils of flame curled below the rafters. It was long past time to go. He took a final look around him at all that remained of his world, and with a choked sob, he slipped out the back entrance and stumbled incautiously into the waiting darkness.

With great difficulty, he forced himself down the long-remembered path to the nearby stream. With any luck he might hide there until the orcs had gone. He waded into the stream, and headed south a short distance to cover his tracks, finally pulling himself out of the water and into a low-hanging tree.

The nightmare was not over. All that night as Andrew hid in the tree, the orcs quartered the area searching for survivors. To aid the search, the monsters led nasty, snarling wolves on long leather leashes. Finally, Andrew was forced to abandon his tree and was driven from one hiding place to another as the orcs beat the bushes and set fire to anything large enough to hide a person.

Andrew had seen Mistress Goody chopped down as she crouched beneath a hayrick, and Master Selwin was spitted by a spear as he clung to the rafters of his smokehouse. A small boy was brought down by the wolves as he attempted to run into the steam. They snapped him up and fought over the scraps.

As Andrew took shelter in a shallow well that had gone dry and been filled to the top with rocks, he was astonished to come face to face with two small children, a boy about ten and a girl of perhaps eight. They stared at him with huge eyes but were too terrified to scream. He recognized them and spoke in a low whisper.

"Young Kirk! And, is that you, Kizzy?" The boy nodded, but the girl just stared at him blankly. Playmates, he remembered, but not brother and sister. They were the children of people he knew to be dead. Without a word, he drew them under his arms, giving them the semblance of protection even though he knew that he could offer them little or nothing.

The well was not a safe place, Andrew realized after a moment's thought. It was too exposed and too obvious a hiding place. The orcs were sure to find them. But it would be difficult to move unseen with the children. Fortunately, the orcs had been unable to consign the contents of the alehouse to the fire and as the night progressed, they became more and more inebriated. The intensity of the search for survivors faded as orcs began staggering about and falling.

Andrew watched with grim satisfaction as several of them began arguing among themselves, hacking and slashing at each other. Only one of them was killed before the leader, a monstrously large creature with a sloped brow and a nose that had been mashed flat at some time in the past, put an end to the fight by chopping the heads off those involved.

During the height of this ruckus, Andrew was able to slip out of the well, followed one at a time by the children. He led them back to his own bit of land, the forge now no more than a glowing skeleton.

By its faint, glimmering light, he led Kirk and Kizzy out to the far edge of the village, where there stood, still unburned, a dense and fragrant bay tree. Andrew hoped, no, he prayed, that its strong scent would cover any sign of their own. To assist matters, he stripped a number of the leaves from the branches and crushed them with his palms, releasing the strong aroma, then dropped the broken leaves to the ground.

Thanks to the rum and ale or the effect of the bay leaves, the three of them escaped detection. They were too afraid to sleep, and huddled together miserably on a large hard branch. For some reason, in the small hours before dawn, the orcs disappeared, withdrew from the ruined town as silently as they had come.

Dawn rose in all its quiet majesty, spreading pearly light, pinks and mauves and roses, illuminating the blackened horror that had once been a peaceful village. Birds sang and butterflies flitted across the gruesome scene. Here and there bits of timber still smoldered and tiny curls of smoke wound upward to be blown away by the gentle morning breeze. It was hard to believe that such horror had occurred the night before. All around them was beauty—birds, butterflies, flowers—it was as though the wanton slaughter had never taken place. But it had.

Andrew's bones ached as he eased himself down to the ground. He turned to the children. "Here now, dearies, 'tis safe enough to come down now, I be thinkin'." He reached up and lifted them down one at a time. The children were silent, their eyes red, their cheeks stained with tears that had carved channels through the smoky grime that clung to their flesh. They were trembling visibly. He led them gently to the pyre that was the end of life as they had known it, their fingers so tiny, so small within his huge grasp. Despite the fear of lurking danger, Andrew knelt to recite a simple prayer, and then, with the children, spoke the names of everyone they could remember.

"Come children, we must be leavin' now." Andrew rose to his feet. "Let's see if we can find any food to take with us." They searched through the rubble that remained, the children numb and wide-eyed. Finally they found a few broken loaves of bread and some cheese and a pair of dull knives. This, Andrew dropped into a cloth sack which he threw over his shoulder. He then led them away toward the cover of the nearby wood.

The days and nights that followed were a blur of fear which, thankfully, they could never quite recall. Afraid of following the open road in case the orcs were near, and terrified of the brambly wilderness that lined the roads, they crept along like frightened rabbits, taking shelter in whatever hidey-hole was big enough to hold them. The bread and cheese was soon gone and they ate whatever they could find—puff balls, mushrooms, berries, grass seeds, and a sweet that Kizzy had knotted in her pocket. They licked the dew from leaves.

In this manner they somehow transversed most of the twenty odd leagues that separated their village from the Castle Elfwood. Always Andrew's fear was tempered by the need for haste. He was driven by the dire necessity to alert those in the castle so that they might spread the alarm and thus protect others from the fate of Fierdras.

It was Kizzy who ended their flight. She had awakened before the others and wandered far from where her companions still slept. At the base of a great rock the girl had found a tiny seepage where spicy cress had taken root.

Kizzy was filling her mouth with the peppery leaves when a leathery hand fell upon her shoulder. Perhaps there were words as well, but she never heard them, so great was her terror. She leaped to her feet with a loud shriek, turning only long enough to sink her teeth into the hand that held her captive, before attempting to make good her escape.

They were sharp little teeth, and the blood ran red down the sun-tanned skin. But despite the curses uttered, the hand only tightened its grip. Kizzy screamed as loud and piercingly as she could and Andrew and Kirk soon came crashing out of the underbrush brandishing sturdy clubs and sharp, pointy rocks.

Kizzy had her eyes squinched shut, wailing at the top of her lungs. She struck out, catching Andrew painfully upon the bridge of his nose as he lifted her and pressed her head against his broad chest. Only there, in the safety of his arms, did Kizzy open her eyes long enough to discover through tear-dewed lashes that her captor was a grizzled captain of the guard from the Castle Elfwood. They were safe at last.

Chapter 9

THE EARL OF ELFWOOD

THE FUNERAL FIRES WERE OUT AND THE COURTYARD HAD BEEN scoured clean. On the surface, Castle Elfwood had returned to normal. But to those in high places, it was a trying time. Jaeme, not ready to become the new lord, or to deal with his father's death, was in a black mood, and barricaded himself in his room refusing to talk to anyone, not even Polonius or his friend Joseph.

The servants left food outside his door as the master-at-arms bade them, and the young earl was not disturbed. The next morning, Polonius noted with interest that some of the food had disappeared overnight. He walked up to the great oak door and knocked twice.

"Jaeme," said the master-at-arms gently. "This is Polonius." He paused, but there was no answer. "I have left you alone long enough. The affairs of state do not stop with the death of one man. There is much you need to learn, and writs and papers to be signed. You will soon be the lord, and must prepare yourself for such responsibilities."

A muffled groan came from within. "Good." Polonius said, smiling to himself. "I shall expect to see you in the library within the hour!'' The master-at-arms turned and walked away, his keys clanking on the chain that hung from his waist.

Inside, Jaeme rolled out of his bed and walked to the window. He stared out at the courtyard unseeing, and sighed, wishing now that he was back in the highland village of Ahtska, where just a short time ago he had been feeling so ill-used. Now he felt even more abused, for soon he was to be Lord of Elfwood.

At length, he turned and headed for the door. An order from Polonius was not to be ignored. Tight-lipped and silent, he made his way through the hallways and up the winding stair that led to his father's library. If he was to be the new Earl of Elfwood, he supposed he had better have some idea of what he was supposed to do.

Several days later Jaeme was awakened rudely by his friend Joseph as the first rays of the morning sun shone in through the one small window in his room. The air was cold and damp and he pulled a bearskin around him as he sat up muttering.

''Hurry, m'lord, there is much to be done this day. The celebrations begin, and you must make ready.'' Two servants followed and began dressing the young earl. Skyler, Jaeme's squire, appeared with a polished breastplate and a sword and scabbard and helped fasten them on.

Most of the next hour was spent in prayer inside the small chapel built out from the side of the inner wall of his rooms. That done, Polonius pulled Jaeme aside to the library and the two devoted themselves to the consuming task of reading through his father's documents. They were at once educating Jaeme on the affairs of state and searching for clues as to those responsible for his father's murder.

Meanwhile there were many comings and goings at the gate, as guests from around the land began to arrive.

Shortly before noon, Joseph and Skyler again interrupted, and Jaeme was summoned to the inner chamber of the lord's hall, where he was surrounded by the remaining knights and all the ladies of Castle Elfwood. Many rushed forward to greet him, for most were old friends and relatives who wanted to wish him well in his new life as lord of the castle. A particularly beautiful young woman came out of the crowd and introduced herself. The name was long and complex, and it immediately left Jaeme's mind the moment she spoke it. Yet his breath was almost taken away by the sight of her beauty—red curls, and deep green eyes, simple dress. Had he met her once before? She stepped forward unbidden, took his hand, and led him wordlessly to the tall wooden chair at the head of the hall.

He would have liked to speak to her, but she disappeared as quickly as she had come, and the young lord saw her no more that day.

The rest of the afternoon was spent in wild celebration, as if nothing terrible had recently happened in the land. It was as though all those around Jaeme were happy that his father was dead and the son was ascending the "throne."

That evening Jaeme was taken to the bathhouse and drenched unceremoniously until he was sparkling clean. Servants came forward to dry him. Then he was dressed in the finest garments of linen and silk, which bore the heraldry of Castle Elfwood. A fine horse, a gift from Edmund, King in Lundinium, was brought into his room, and Jaeme was amazed. Never in his life had he seen such an animal. It was grey in color and peaceful in disposition, yet its legs were firm and strong. It was clearly a horse that could support a knight in full armour and still be quite agile in battle.

Jaeme waved the animal and its keepers away, intent upon proceeding with the ceremonies that would establish him permanently as the Seventh Earl of Elfwood—an honor he was still not ready to receive, but anxious to have so that he could get on with his program of revenge.

The next morning Jaeme was armed with corselets of double-woven mail which no lance or arrow could pierce, and then shod with silver boots girded with golden spurs. A shield portraying a forest of trees was hung around his neck, and a helmet was placed on his head, one of finest polished steel.

Finally, from deep within the many chambers which honeycombed the ground beneath Castle Elfwood, Polonius brought Jaeme a jeweled sword of such fine workmanship that his breath was taken away the moment he cast his eyes upon it.

''Truly fit for a king,'' commented Joseph, who stood by Jaeme's side admiring the weapon.

''I shall only become the Earl of Elfwood, remember.''

''Well then, fit for an earl . . . and if you decide you don't need this, I'm sure I could find a use for it.''

Jaeme took the sword and made a few passes at an invisible opponent. ''It has a nice feel, and good balance. I wonder why my father never used it himself?''

''Your father,'' said Polonius very seriously, ''won that sword some years before you were born, in battle with Valgran in the Pictish Wastes.'' The master-at-arms took the sword from Jaeme, walked over to the window, and held it in the sunlight. ''You'll notice when the sun is right, there are strange inscriptions along the blade, and more here across the hilt. We knew this sword was not of Albion, and your father believed it had magic within, for it made him uneasy when he attempted to carry it. He put it in a box, and when we returned, I took it to be examined by the Royal Wizard at Lundinium. He was unable to read the writings but said that the sword was of Byzantine origins and was indeed endowed with magic of the good kind.'' Polonius returned the sword to Jaeme, who now regarded it with even more awe.

''Your father bade me store it in the dungeons below the castle against the time that he might have a son. That came to pass. . . . So you see, Jaeme, this is a gift from your father, Richard, but 'twas not to be given until after his death.''

''I am deeply honored.''

A bell rang and messengers appeared at the door. Jaeme was led out into the lower bailey, where an enormous crowd was packed inside the castle walls. In an open space in the centre was a raised platform, upon which stood the local cleric and several others of the church. Polonius led his young charge past the adoring throngs amid murmurs and shouts of congratulations. The old master-at-arms was pleased to see young Jaeme so received, yet filled with sorrow that his beloved Richard was now gone. He was not at all sure the young lad could fill his father's shoes.

Chapter 10
THE COUNCIL

"MAY I INTRODUCE THE NEW, OFFICIAL AMBASSADOR FROM THE Druids of the Wood, Laelestequenstrutia." The long and convoluted name rolled sonorously through the vast, high-vaulted room. Polonius' pronunciation was flawless. A smile twitched at the corners of Laela's lips and she winked at the greybeard, causing him to flush a deep, dark red and burst into a fit of coughing. She had discovered the effect that she had on the old man by accident, catching him staring at her with open admiration in an unguarded moment. Flirting with him was one of the few pleasures she had discovered in the day and a half she had spent in the gloomy castle.

Laela lifted her head proudly. She was dressed in a green gown that had been acquired from one of the ladies-in-waiting, useless creatures who seemed to have no purpose but to gather in gaggles to giggle and whisper. Since she had lost all of her possessions during the affray with the black riders in the woods, Polonius had insisted that she wear this gown for the presentation to the new Earl of Elfwood.

Poor Polonius, he had not seen anything wrong with the

dress, but Laela had discovered that numerous seams were torn apart, stressed it would seem by a too-large body confined within the soft velvet. Nor had it been clean. There was a large egg stain worked deep into the fabric and the skirt was faded in patches. Laela had thanked Polonius prettily and then set to work, mending the torn fabric, altering it to fit her smaller, more slender frame and then managed to clean it by gently sponging it with a potion of leaves and flowers gathered from the garden.

When she was done, it was far lovelier than when it was new. The dress now hugged her slender body as though it had been designed with her in mind. The potion had an added bonus. As the fabric swung gracefully about her long legs, it cast an almost phosphorescent glow that hung in the wake of her passage for a few seconds before dispersing.

Laela's perfume was an elusive fragrance. Also made from flowers she had gathered, it tantalized and teased the nostrils of those she passed, leaving them casting about in the air like hunting dogs after a mysterious scent, yearning for more.

She passed through the ranks of those who had gathered in the Great Hall, head held high, hearing their whispers, knowing that she could not name one among them as a friend. She would not like this place, that she knew, but she also knew her responsibilities. The link between the Folk of the Wood and Elfwood Castle was an old one, the oldest alliance between Druids and the men of the outside world. It was a singular honor, especially for one as young as she; she would not be found faulting, no matter how onerous the task.

She traversed the long hall, the crowds dressed in all their finery parting before her. Her feet and legs were clad in knee-high green velvet boots which she had fashioned out of the excess material. Laela would have preferred to go barefoot, but Polonius had been clearly shocked at the suggestion, and she did not have the heart to provoke him.

She ascended the steps to the top of the podium where the young Earl sat and, bending one velvet-clad knee, she knelt and dipped her head to show her allegiance. The whispers raced through the hall like a swarm of angry wasps, and Laela hid her amusement beneath the cover of her red curls. She knew it was unseemly for a woman to kneel in such a manner—only men knelt, women curtseyed—but Laela could not abide curtseys, thought them too smarmy for words. This would give the busybodies something to talk about!

"Ha, hem!" Someone cleared his throat loudly, and Laela rose and stood before the earl with head held high, her eyes meeting and holding his. He grinned openly and Laela grinned back. Hmmm, she thought, maybe this won't be so bad after all. She studied him frankly, noting that he had grown greatly since their last meeting. He was tall, very tall, and still not comfortable with it from the awkward way he slouched in his chair, obviously uncertain about what to do with his gangly legs.

His long, straight nose was handsome and his eyes were nice, possibly the nicest thing about him—dark, black, even, and melancholy, fringed with thick silky lashes. They burned with an intensity that was old beyond his years, and a hint of grief as well. But there was sincerity and honesty in those eyes, and in that moment Laela knew that this was a human she could respect and perhaps even honor. She put away all memory of the time he had pulled her hair as a youth, and all the anger she had stored up for him on her trip to the castle. He would need a bit of guidance, but then, she thought as she turned a dazzling smile on him, that should not prove a difficult task.

Polonius had joined her on the dais and spoke at great length about the relationship between the castle and the Wood. Jaeme made the appropriate noises and Laela murmured from time to time. Finally, much to her relief, all was said and done and Laela took what would be her official position at the earl's right hand.

She had not known that there were to be other announcements and she was somewhat startled when Polonius boomed out another name, one Decutonius Consulus. Laela thought it a rather pompous name and was prepared to see an old, fat merchant waddle forward. She was therefore more than a little surprised when a young man in his early twenties began the long walk down the center of the hall. She was even more surprised to hear Polonius proclaim him to be the new mage appointed to the court by the Great Wizard of Lundinium.

Laela stared at him in amazement. This was a mage? Why, he was a mere boy, probably still an apprentice! How could one as young as he be entrusted with such a heavy responsibility? Never for a moment did Laela stop to think that she herself was far younger than the mage she had already taken an instant dislike to. Lewtt flittered beneath her curls, then tugged on one to get her attention, but Laela was too interested in watching the young man approach the dais to pay attention to the sprite.

Almost as though she had planted the idea in his mind, Jaeme turned to Polonius and asked in a low tone, "Since when do we need a mage from Lundinium amongst us?"

Still smiling benevolently at young Dec, Polonius replied without moving his lips: "Your father personally sent for a mage, requesting the help of the Wizard. Perhaps he realized that dark times lay ahead."

"Oh . . . of course . . ." Jaeme fell silent at the mention of his father, a bleak look crossing his face. He studied the young man in the long blue robe who stood uncertainly before the throne. Although doing his best to conceal his discomfort, it was obvious that he was ill at ease.

"Pleased to be at your service, m'lord." Dec made an awkward bow. Jaeme sighed. He could scarcely hold the fellow's youth against him; he himself was no older, and already the earl in a land he was hardly ready to rule. He made welcoming noises to take some of the tension out of the air.

"Umm, and how was your journey to our fine land, Deku . . . ? I'm sorry, I haven't quite mastered the name."

"Decutonius Consulus!" said Polonius helpfully.

"Dec, just call me Dec, please." Polonius motioned for him to be seated in a chair opposite Jaeme and he did so. "My journey. Well, it was great, quite a fine adventure, I suppose. That is, all except for the attack of the Northmen, of course. It was my first time on a ship." He was unprepared for the reaction to his words.

"Attack of the Northmen?" Polonius and Jaeme spoke as one, the young earl rising half out of his chair.

"Well, yes," Dec said in confusion. Had he said something wrong? "We were attacked by Northmen, three nasty longboats they were. Full of the ugliest, smelliest bunch I've ever seen. They nearly got us, but I threw some lightning bolts and blasted them out of the water." The number of ships had grown in his memory, and wisely, he left off all mention of half-destroying his own ship in the process.

Jaeme and Polonius turned to each other, shock and

dismay written on their faces. "I thought that King Edmund had vanquished the Northmen as well as the pirates in our waters," Jaeme said slowly.

"It was my understanding as well," Polonius agreed. "Are you quite certain, young man, that these were Northmen?"

Dec described the ships, the snakelike prows and the dress and look of the men manning the oars. When he had finished his report, there was no doubt in anyone's minds that the attackers were indeed Northmen.

"Perhaps it was but a rogue band, m'lord," Polonius offered. "There have been no other reports of trouble on the seas."

"I hate to differ with you," Dec said slowly, "but the captain was worried before we ever left port. He said that there had been lots of trouble of late with both pirates and Northmen."

The two men stared at one another, digesting this bit of unwelcome news. The court hummed with whispers and snatches of excited conversations. Jaeme became aware of the many eyes and ears focused on the dais. This would not do. There was too much that was unexplained already without adding fuel to the fire. With a wave of his hand, he dismissed the court, wondering at the ease of the gesture, and whether he would ever get used to being able to direct the lives of so many people with just a flick of his finger. The members of the court filed out with many a backward glance, obviously unhappy at missing out on whatever else was to be divulged.

When the last of them had passed through the broad doors at the end of the hall, Laela leaned forward and spoke.

"I also had an unfriendly encounter upon my journey to Castle Elfwood. It happened as I travelled through the

Wood.'' All eyes turned to her. With a few well-chosen words, she described the band of intruders she had met in the forest and detailed the terrible destruction they had visited upon her beloved wilds.

There was a long moment of silence as the four of them regarded each other with solemn eyes.

Polonius was the first to speak. ''What can this mean?'' ''If it were simply a matter of Northmen or of vandals in the forest, one could perhaps explain it in some manner, but coupled with the villainous attack on your father . . . I'm afraid it must all tie together. Someone or something is behind it, but who or what?''

''Who has reason to want my father dead?'' Jaeme asked darkly. He answered his own question in the next breath. ''Felker,'' he said broodingly. ''It can be no other.''

''Who is this Felker?'' Dec asked. ''And why would he want your father dead?''

''Felker is the Lord of Harrowhall,'' replied Polonius. ''In name he owes fealty to the Earl of Elfwood. His lands lie to the south and his holding quite extensive, but I think I reveal no secrets when I say that he is known to openly covet Elfwood and has often opined that he would would've ruled it better than our dear, late Richard.''

''He is a spineless, conniving rat!'' Jaeme said with feeling. ''And he had the audacity to bring gifts and attend the funeral. I know it was Felker! Who else could it be?''

''My lord, far be it for me to say that you are wrong,'' Polonius said smoothly, ''but we live in uneasy times, and much as I dislike the man, I cannot ignore the fact that there are many others capable of such deeds.''

''Who?'' asked Dec when it appeared obvious that Jaeme was not going to ask.

''Foremost among those I would suspect is another lord,

one Penwarden,'' said Polonius. Jaeme growled. The master-at-arms-continued. ''He occupies a castle not too distant from our own. He too is a vassal of this court, but I believe the man has . . . aspirations.'' Much emphasis was placed on the single word. It was easy to conclude that this Penwarden was no favorite of the old man. Dec and Laela exchanged glances over the head of the young earl whom they had both sworn to uphold and protect. It appeared that the job would entail more than either of them had suspected.

They were deep in conversation, discussing the black tunics with the yellow diamond, which Laela had described as an afterthought. It seemed to cause much consternation between Jaeme and Polonius. They had queried Dec backward and forward on the subject, prying at his memory to learn if any of the Northmen had been dressed in such a tunic. Dec had steadfastly denied seeing any such tunics, and was describing the attackers garb when the doors to the hall were suddenly flung apart, striking the stone walls and creating a resounding echo in the empty hall.

The small group looked up at the noise, wondering at the interruption. Jaeme rose, clearly annoyed at having his orders disobeyed. He was frowning. A fierce, dark look had come over his handsome features, and Laela shivered, realizing suddenly that this young man was not to be taken too lightly. There was steel beneath the disarming manner.

She peered into the shadows that had filled the hall, and gasped in alarm. Her eyes, perhaps sharper than those around her, or perhaps merely accustomed to following the swift movement of animals in the dim forest light, had spied out what the men on the dais had yet to see.

Hurrying toward them were two castle guards, escorting a large, muscular, half-naked young man and two young children. Their clothes were torn and filthy, and their skin bore signs of blood, smoke, and exposure. Laela's fingers dug into the decorative strip of wood at the top of her chair. Whatever news this was, it would not be good.

"Beggin' yer pardon to be disturbing ya, m'lord," said one of the guards tentatively, "but we thought as this was fairly important news this man brings."

Polonius blanched as the small group emerged from the shadows. Jaeme's eyes opened wide, all signs of anger wiped away. He hurried down the steps without a moment's thought to his position and helped the children into chairs. It was clear that they were near collapse. Laela needed no urging to take herself to the side of the children. Their eyes were huge with the wonder of actually being inside the castle they had heard so many tales about, much less tended to by the earl himself. But their eyes also held ghosts of fear that were not so easily banished.

"Bring more chairs!" Jaeme commanded, and the guards hurried off. Andrew refused to sit despite his exhaustion, and would have knelt before his lord, but Jaeme would have none of it. A compromise was reached when Jaeme leaped up the steps of the dais and impatiently tugged the heavy throne, *kerblang, kerblang, kerblang,* down the steps and positioned himself directly in front of Andrew's chair, commanding him with an imperious bend of his finger to sit himself down. Andrew obeyed with a weak smile.

The story came out in a tumble of words. First Andrew spoke, then Kirk, interrupted by Kizzy whose words were somewhat distorted by the fact that two of her front teeth were missing (due to natural causes). Suddenly, she began to cry. Then, through streaming tears, she told of seeing her family killed. It seemed that she had been one of a large brood of children. She was the only survivor.

Kirk's tale was no less traumatic, but he managed to contain his tears even though his eyes shone unnaturally bright. When he finished his sad story, he formally requested a favor of Jaeme.

"Of course, young Kirk, if it is in my power to grant it, you have but to ask."

"I want to be a soldier," Kirk said solemnly. "I want to hunt down them dirty orcs and kill them like they killed the people of Fierdras. Give me a sword and I'll kill them all!" His small body was trembling with the fervor of his words.

Jaeme's first instinct was to take the boy on his knee and tell him nicely that he was too young. But the look in the boy's eye stopped him. Instead, he cast a glance at Polonius, who nodded knowingly. Jaeme sank to one knee in front of the boy.

"Kirk, I would value your arm and your allegiance at my side. But you would serve me and the memory of your parents better if you would accept a bit of training first. Can you delay being a soldier for just a little while?" Kirk looked into the eyes of his lord, who was really just another grownup when you came down to it, to see if he was being condescended to. What he read there convinced him that the earl was sincere. He nodded solemnly. Jaeme offered his hand. Kirk slipped his own small hand into Jaeme's and they sealed their bargain. As Jaeme rose, he had the odd feeling that this was not the last he would hear of young Kirk.

Jaeme then beckoned one of the men-at-arms who had escorted the trio. "Take this boy. Find him a bed in the dormitory, find him suitable clothes and weapons. Tomorrow he will take his place among those who would train to be knights in my service."

The guards exchanged startled glances. This was an

honor reserved for the sons of lords and other high-ranking nobles. And their parents were expected to pay for the privilege, which took many, many years. It was unheard of for a common peasant, much less an orphaned peasant, to be accorded such an honor. They eyed young Kirk with new regard.

Laela, during the exchange between Kirk and the earl, had drawn Lewtt out of her curls like a magician drawing a coin out of his ear. She offered him to Kizzy, whose eyes and mouth opened wide. Dec too, watched in amazement, never having seen a wood sprite before. The tiny creature, accepting an unspoken command from Laela, immediately set about amusing the little girl. First, he flittered up to her teary eyes and wiped them with a tiny handkerchief which he produced from heavens knew where. Then he dried her cheeks with fast flutters of his wings, which produced a chorus of giggles as they tickled back and forth. He pretended to stub his toe on her freckled nose and tumbled head over heels, causing Kizzy to shriek in alarm and catch him in her grubby little hand.

I would only do this for you, Laelestequenstrutia! complained Lewtt silently to his mistress. He then amused the child with a number of dazzling aerial maneuvers and ended by perching on the tip of her slightly uptilted nose, causing her bright blue eyes to cross. Laela lifted him gently. The sprite bowed to the little girl, who smiled prettily, stood up, and curtseyed neatly in return. Lewtt shot Laela a doleful glance, having obviously had enough of all this.

''Can I sleep with him tonight?'' Kizzy asked, eyes shining with adoration.

''Yes, but only for tonight,'' Laela replied, shooting a startled Lewtt a look of her own.

Andrew was praised for his bravery and the courageous rescue of the children.

"I could have done naught else, my lord," Andrew replied simply.

"What will you do now?" asked Jaeme. "Do you have family elsewhere?"

"No, my lord. Everyone I had lived in Fierdras."

"Then I hope that I may persuade you to remain here in the castle. You did a neat bit of work on my stallion the time he split his hoof. We can use a man of your talents. Please consider. We would be honored to have you."

The words, spoken humbly and honestly from one man to the other, carried the weight of sincerity and conviction. Andrew bowed stiffly before the young lord and tugged his forelock in allegiance. Jaeme reached out and grasped the smithy's hand and shoulder. He looked into Andrew's eyes.

"Thank you, my friend, for your actions. With such men as you behind me, we shall prevail against all who would stand against us."

When they were alone in the huge hall, Jaeme, Dec, Laela, and Polonius looked at each other worriedly. Obviously they were being drawn into something bigger and blacker than any of them had envisioned.

Polonius sighed, looking dispirited and frail, an elderly man carrying the burdens of state on his shoulders with only a young and inexperienced earl to aid him along with a mage and a Druidess who were equally young and untried.

"My lord," he said quietly. "What will you do?"

"It's a conspiracy, it seems clear enough," Jaeme replied. "First they killed my father, then they stirred the Northmen into action. The destruction of the forest. And now this attack by the orcs. What will it be next?" The young earl had spoken softly, as though to himself. Now he raised his eyes to his companions and they could see that those dark orbs were blazing.

The master-at-arms nodded agreement. "It would indeed seem to be a conspiracy."

"Someone thinks I'm too young. With my father gone, they thought everything would fall apart and they would be there to pick up the pieces." Jaeme turned to Laela, seized her hand in a feverish grip, and pulled her toward him. "Are you with me?" he asked, searching her eyes with his own, looking at her with such intensity that she felt as though he were boring into her soul. "I want to hunt them down, those filthy, murdering orcs. I must make it clear that I stand by my people in their hour of need, just as they come when I command. The orcs must be hunted down, every last one of them, and slain as a message to all my enemies. As Lord of the Castle Elfwood, I must stand firm. Will you aid me?"

Laela felt as though the air was being sucked out of her lungs. She could not break away from the young lord's gaze, his eyes held her fast. She could do naught but nod her head. Only then did he release her and turn to Polonius, firing orders at the old man, faster than he could possibly scribble them down. He began to stride down the hall, still shouting directives over his shoulder.

"Wait!" cried Dec. "What about me?" That he seemed to have been left out of the plans disturbed him more than he might have imagined. A small boy, a smith, and a Druid had been personally invited by Jaeme to take part in what was to come. But what about him? Dec was well aware that he had created nothing but trouble in his overly long career as a student mage, but suddenly he wanted more than anything he had ever wanted before, to help, to be a part of whatever it was that was happening here. He knew that he was more accustomed to making mischief than magic, but

THEY didn't know that. This was serious. This was real. If he tried hard, he could do it, something important that might turn the tide of battle or power. They just had to give him a chance!

Jaeme stopped in mid-stride, turned abruptly, and looked at Dec, who had leaped off the dais and run after the lord whom he had been sent to aid. He all but skidded into him, so suddenly did he stop.

"Do I need to issue you a special invitation, mage?" Jaeme said with a lopsided grin. "That would be like inviting a man to enter his own home; you are, after all, the Wizard of Elfwood."

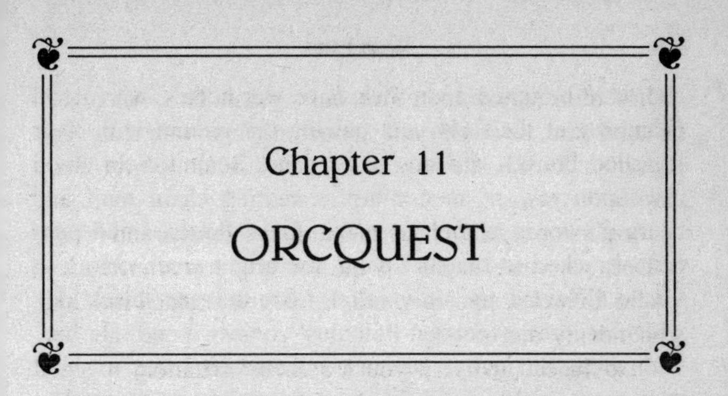

Chapter 11
ORCQUEST

THE MORNING DAWNED GREY AND GLOOMY WITH LOW, DARK clouds scudding across the threatening sky. The sun was nowhere to be seen. There was a cruel edge to the wind which carried the threat of winter in its sibilant whisper. From the look of the heavy-bellied clouds, hail or even snow seemed likely, though it was but the middle of summer.

Jaeme had acted swiftly on the news he had received from Andrew and the children. Already, even though the cocks were still abed with their heads tucked beneath their wings, every fighting man available had been mustered forth, provisioned, and was ready to march.

Polonius had tried to dissuade Jaeme from such a hasty course of action, but the young earl had swept his arguments aside. He had been burning to strike out against whoever had been responsible for his father's death, and although it was unlikely that the orcs had had any part in that terrible deed, Jaeme, in the impulsiveness of youth, saw his action, any action, as better than sitting still and doing nothing.

The few remaining knights had been gathered together

and were mounted upon their huge war horses, who stood champing at their bits and pawing the ground with their ironshod hooves, anxious to be gone. Behind them stood row upon row of men-at-arms, wearing chain mail and bearing swords as well as pikes. Flags fluttered and pennants cracked in the stiff wind, the bright green colors of Castle Elfwood the only relief from the grey-black day which accurately echoed Polonius' somber mood. He had, with great difficulty, persuaded Jaeme to leave a small contingent at the castle. It was not that he was personally afraid, but it did not seem wise to leave the castle defenseless.

"All right, old man, you shall have your guard!" Jaeme had finally agreed angrily.

They stood now upon the ramparts, surveying the gathered troops, discussing the running of affairs in Jaeme's absence, Polonius raising small, inconsequential matters in an attempt to forestall the inevitable. He could not rid himself of the certainty that Jaeme's plan would end in disaster. He had an awful, fluttery sick feeling in the pit of his stomach that told him so.

An advisor who had reached his lofty position was supposed to rely on fact and other bits of solid information in reaching his conclusions, but over the years Polonius had learned that the fluttery feeling in his stomach was never wrong.

"At least postpone your departure," he pleaded, daring to incur more of Jaeme's wrath. Already the young earl's face was set in angry lines. "I beg you, wait for reinforcements from your liege lords . . . a bigger force. . . ."

Jaeme spun on his heel and began to pace. For the first time in his life, *he* was lording it over Polonius. He tried to control his temper, realizing that the old man was only doing what he thought best. He took a deep breath before he spoke. "Sir, it is imperative that we leave now while the trail is fresh. As you can see, the weather threatens. A good heavy rainstorm could obliterate the trail completely."

Polonius all but wrung his hands. "And what if the army who slew your father chooses to attack the castle in your absence?"

Jaeme continued calmly. "That will not happen. You heard Laela. She met those men in the Wood and set them upon each other. They are no longer a matter of concern."

He might have said more, would certainly have done so, but at that moment they were interrupted by the arrival of Jaeme's squire, Skyler, breathless from having taken the stairs two and three at a time in his haste to reach them. Between gasps, he reported that a large army had appeared and was now positioned in front of the castle.

Polonius threw Jaeme a look that was at once apprehensive and reproachful. Jaeme blanched, and reeled as though he had been struck. Almost before Skyler had finished his report, the young earl was running along the narrow edge of the rampart, his long legs carrying him at a pace Polonius could not hope to match on his own aged, shaking limbs.

When the master-of-arms finally caught up with Jaeme at the front of the castle, he could see that the squire had spoken the truth. Stretching away from the edge of the river to the very top of the next hill was a large army, armed to the teeth with all manner of weapons.

With sinking heart and a powerful flutter in his stomach, Polonius recognized the red and black colors of Harrowhall. It was Felker! Their suspicions had been correct after all. Knowing that he and Jaeme had correctly guessed the villain's identity scarcely made imminent defeat more palatable. Polonius' mouth was filled with bitterness.

Strangely, Jaeme did not seem to realize the full import of Felker's arrival. At this very moment, he was leaning over the edge of the wall, shouting down to Felker, who sat astride his fat war horse, a huge smile on his darkly tanned face. Hatred stabbed at Polonius, twisting inside him. He was basically a man of peace, but at this moment he wanted nothing more than to smash that smug smile off Felker's face. Richard had been as a son to him, and he knew in his heart—and his stomach—that he was looking at a murderer.

Polonius shook off his black thoughts, suddenly aware of the words that were being spoken. To his amazement, he heard Jaeme speaking in a friendly manner and Felker replying in kind!

"We have come to march by your side 'gainst the vile orcs!" Felker shouted in a deep voice.

"Your arrival is timely indeed, Lord Felker!" replied Jaeme. "Even now the armies of Castle Elfwood are ready to depart. Meet me at the gate!" Felker waved. His horse snorted and whirled round, and made at a trot for the entrance. Polonius all but reeled at this exchange.

"No, wait, Jaeme my son." Polonius extended a shaking hand, frail, paper-white, and spotted with age. He clutched Jaeme's sleeve as he started to run past to descend the stairs and welcome Felker. "You cannot go off with this man! Look, his forces are so much greater than your own, you could be easily overpowered! Think! This man is the enemy!"

Jaeme turned to Polonius, removing his hand gently but with a show of impatience. "This man *may* be the enemy. I am no fool, nor am I a child who cannot reason for himself," he said in clipped tones. "I agree, Felker is the first choice for the one responsible for those heinous acts, but he can scarcely cause mischief if he is riding at my side! And the orcs are an enemy common to us both!"

"But, my lord, his numbers . . ." Polonius could not hide the quaver that came into his voice. Jaeme did not answer, but descended the stone stair rapidly with his sword clanking at his side.

Later, after some discussion between Jaeme and Felker, the young lord rode back through the gate and spoke to his master-at-arms "Felker has agreed to leave a large garrison behind to help protect the castle."

"But—" Polonius began to protest.

Jaeme cut him short. "That will reduce his numbers substantially and strengthen the castle. That should make you feel better."

Never had Polonius felt so old, so helpless. Had he been a younger, stronger man, he would have burst out of the gates, challenging Felker to a duel, man to man, sword to sword. But he was no longer young. He was an old man and even when he was young, he had never been particularly gifted with arms. His weapons were words, and at the moment, his quiver was empty. He could think of none that would prevent this dreadful alliance. Jaeme spurred his horse to leave.

"Wait, my lord!" Polonius said in desperation. Jaeme was already several steps down and turned to face him, not bothering to erase the look of impatience that tugged the corner of his mouth downward with displeasure.

"Do you not think it odd that Lord Felker has learned of the destruction of Fierdras so soon? After all, we have only just heard of it ourselves. How is it that he is here, outfitted, provisioned, and ready to go on such short notice?"

"You are too suspicious, Polonius," Jaeme said quietly. "You see dangers where none exist. There is such a thing as being too cautious. No doubt there is a simple explanation for all of your questions. It is likely that there were other survivors. If Andrew the Smith and little Kizzy and Kirk escaped, others could have done so as well. Perhaps it did not take them so long to cover the distance. Travelling with children would have slowed Andrew down. News reached Harrowhall instead of Elfwood, thus Felker's presence. No one wants orcs about in the land. It is in his interests as well as ours to drive them out.'' He paused briefly. ''Now, are there any more objections?''

''No, my lord,'' Polonius said softly and Jaeme turned without a backward glance, rode out through the dark castle gate, and halted alongside Felker, men and flags mingling as the two armies joined. Polonius reclimbed the stair, and watched from his perch on the ramparts as the two armies filed away. He could not rid himself of the fear that had filled his belly since Jaeme announced his decision to set forth in pursuit of the orcs. Nothing he had heard or seen since that moment had eased the terrible conviction that his young lord was setting off on a most dangerous mission. He had done and said everything he could to prevent it, and he had failed. He was filled with sadness. What good was an advisor whose advice was not taken? He answered his own question: no good at all.

Jaeme would not have admitted it, but he too was concerned with all the issues that Polonius had raised. However, it seemed to him that riding alongside Felker was a calculated risk, one that he would just have to take. He would much rather have an enemy at his elbow than plotting unseen. He was sorry that he had spoken harshly to Polonius, but he knew that nothing he could have said would have eased the old man's fears. He would have to mend those fences when he returned. It would help if they returned victorious. Then Polonius would see that he had been right.

Part of the problem was that the old man still saw him as a child, not as the lord of the castle. That was another thing that would have to change. Jaeme was anxious to secure this victory for more personal reasons. No one needed to believe in his ability to fill his father's throne more than he himself. Driving the orcs from the land would go a long way toward achieving that goal. Jaeme was determined to succeed.

Still inside the castle, near the rear of the procession, Laela and Decutonius were also struggling with their own set of flutters, each for very different reasons. Laela had serious misgivings about setting forth on a mission of war. Nor was she certain that it was within the parameters of her role to do so. She had been told that she was to act as the liason between the Druids of the Wood and the folk of the castle. There had never been any mention of taking part in a bloodbath such as certainly would occur when this huge army caught up with the orcs.

Laela had no love for orcs. But Druids were known to revere all life and certainly the life of animals. And even as they had absolutely no interest in the affairs and wars of man, they were most definitely against the slaughter of any animals by men. But that was the crux of the problem. What exactly *were* orcs? They were neither animals nor men. They were an abomination, a hideous combination of the very worst of both species. They had no redeeming features and were hated and reviled by Druids as well as men. Did that mean that taking part in a mission to destroy them would be acceptable to her superiors? Laela honestly did not know, but she thought it possible.

Lewtt was suddenly buzzing angrily around her head. *Never again, mistress. Never*! he exclaimed in his tiny voice. He had returned from his evening with Kizzy in a terrible temper. Laela could all but see the dark cloud hanging over his head. A head whose hair was braided in a score of tiny braids, the ends tied with bits of brilliantly colored silk embroidery thread. His face was also colored, his cheeks and lips an unnatural cherry-red and his eyelids a shocking shade of blue. He had obviously attempted to scrub the colors from his face but had merely managed to smear them, giving him a very odd appearance.

Laela, taken by surprise, had made the mistake of bursting into giggles at the strange sight. Now he was perched atop her head, clinging to her locks. She could not dislodge him and all attempts at conciliation met with stony silence. She knew she could not expect any help from Lewtt until he calmed down. She would have to make her own decision about accompanying Jaeme.

In the end, even though the mission had little to do with the relationship between the Wood and the castle, Laela decided to throw her lot in with Jaeme. Her reasoning was thus: orcs were horrible, a menace to every living thing in their path. If they could annihilate an entire village and all the life it held, including animals, was anyone or anything safe? They were highly unpredictable creatures and could just as easily decide to enter the forest and slay her people, or proceed on to Castle Elfwood and lay siege to the folk within. If she aided in their destruction, it could be argued that she was indeed acting on behalf of both the castle and the Wood.

Satisfied with the soundness of her logic and pleased with herself, Laela settled back in her saddle and waited for her turn to ride out the gate. Maybe this ambassador business wasn't so bad after all!

Dec's reservations were of a more earthbound sort. Very

earthbound. The horse he had been given had taken an instant dislike to him, hated him upon sight, and had done everything within its power to kill him. Dec had little or no experience with horses and had viewed the immense red beast with dismay. In his first attempt to mount, the horse's head had snaked back and given him an extremely painful bite on the southernmost portion of his anatomy. The groom had thought it extremely humorous, and it was some time before he could stop laughing long enough to give Dec a hand up into the saddle.

The ground had seemed terribly far away, but that problem had soon been solved when the horse suddenly reared, flinging Dec out of the saddle and onto the very ground he had yearned for only seconds before. Of course he had landed on that already painful southernmost portion of his anatomy, which now hurt even more. And of course there hadn't been any time for thoughts of his old levitation trick. All further attempts to rise into the saddle were met with other inventive moves devised by the beast's malicious mind. It had become quite a show, Decutonius the Daring, Decutonius the Dumb! And a crowd of people, including Laela had gathered to watch.

The score was Decutonius—0, horse—5, when Laela finally stepped in. She hopped lightly down from her mount and fixed the grooms with a nasty look which sent them slinking back to their masters, posthaste. Then, taking the demonic horse by the ear, she whispered words that Dec could not hear for the painful ringing inside his head.

Whatever the words, the horse underwent a miraculous transformation, from creature out of the pits of hell to an obedient, noble steed. Fearing some sort of diabolical trick, Decutonius mounted very cautiously, keeping a careful eye on the horse, ready to leap clear at the slightest twitch of its flank. The horse stood rock-still. Just to make sure, Dec nudged it with his knees. The animal quietly walked around in a circle. Then he pulled it to halt. The horse obeyed his every command.

Dec was impressed. Not only was this Laela beautiful, she was talented as well. Unfortunately, she didn't seem to recognize him as a person. She would have paid more attention to him if he'd been a tree. And now she'd been forced to rescue him from his own horse. How humiliating!

As important as these matters were, there were other, more serious concerns. Firstly, he was extremely nervous about how he would do in the coming encounter. Other than the incident on board ship which, if one was generous, could be called a success, the only real experience he had to his credit was a series of pranks. Oh, true, he had blown up several laboratories and the school—one couldn't forget that—and a wing of his own house as well, but those were all unintentional, if educational in their own way. Dec was very worried that when the time came, he wouldn't be up to the seriousness of the task.

He had been up all night, feverishly reviewing all of his spells, and had packed and repacked his bag, trying to make certain he had all the components he was likely to need.

For the first time in his young life, Dec felt at a loss. Unsure of himself, he wished desperately that he had paid more attention to those very teachers he'd had such a grand time making sport of.

One's first encounter with the harshness of reality is always a humbling, bitter experience, and it was humbling and bitter indeed. He had chortled when old Blubbermouth had turned crimson and told him, "One day, mark my words, you'll wish you'd listened to me." He had guffawed when old Turtle Toes had stormed out of the lab, his hair a wreath of smoking wisps, ranting, "Decutonius, you will rue this day, spending your time playing jokes rather than on your lessons." Dec had roared with laughter when scrawny old Master Sneath had promised him that "One day ya'll git yer comeuppance!" Dec sighed. The day they all predicted loomed large in the near future.

At last the time came and Dec followed Laela out the gate and on to the beginning of his career as the Mage of Elfwood.

The first day the army marched at a fast pace west by north along the road that had once been Offa's Wall. By the time they made camp that night, Dec was sore all over, in spite of the gentle cooperation he had received from his horse. He had just dismounted and was rubbing his backside and groaning, when a messenger arrived inviting both him and Laela to the campfire of the lords.

Round a large crackling fire sat the leaders of the great expedition, tended by their servants. Dec was shown to a seat on a log that was covered with twigs sticking out in all directions. He declined and plopped down on the soft grass. He was then introduced to Lord Felker, a heavy dark man with a thick black mustache and an oily personality. Dec took an immediate dislike to the man.

"So, you're the new Mage of Elfwood I've heard so much about." Felker grinned. Dec was sure he detected a note of sarcasm in his voice. "News of your adventure on the high seas precedes you." Felker smiled and nodded his head in a little bow of respect.

There was an awkward moment of silence, and all eyes turned to Dec. He was expected to answer. "Oh, uh, it was all in a day's work, m'lord. Just ordinary stuff, really." Dec swallowed hard. The weasel-eyed man in the orange robe sitting next to Felker raised his eyebrows at that last remark.

Felker grinned—too much. "You will, of course, have much to discuss with my own magician"—he waved his hand toward weasel-eyes—"Gratten, the Red Mage of Harrowhall." Dec and Gratten nodded at each other, saying nothing. From the very first moment the two of them laid eyes on one another, war had been declared. It was a silent war—nothing was said—but it was a war nonetheless.

There was an air of evil and corruption about the man that was so strong Dec was surprised that everyone could not feel it. Not even Laela, whom he would have thought to be sensitive to such a powerful aura, showed any sign of distrust. But she was seated some distance away and seemed somewhat distracted, dealing with that sprite of hers who was still decked out in a very odd fashion. Perhaps she would notice Gratten later.

Dec was more than a little worried about Gratten. Not only was the man a much older and therefore a more practiced mage, but he seemed to regard Dec with the same degree of esteem one would have for a particularly loathsome bug. He kept his eye on Dec at all times, a sneer on his lips and a look in his eye not unlike that of Dec's horse before its transformation.

Dec became convinced that Gratten was up to something, for he kept rubbing his hands together in a strange repetitive motion. Dec began to weave a spell of safekeeping around himself, reasoning that Gratten would have to dispose of him first if he had intentions on the group. Damn! he thought to himself, if I had only listened more closely to Squintum on the day he covered this spell.

Dec was dismayed to note that Jaeme seemed totally taken with Felker, who was, in Dec's opinion, only a shade less dangerous than his mage. Later, just as they were going off to sleep, Laela spoke to him, having finally reached some kind of agreement with her little companion. He was glad to learn that she shared his opinion on both Felker and Gratten.

Two days had passed since their leavetaking from the castle. Both Dec and Laela had grown somewhat closer in that they shared a common worry. At their every attempt to speak to Jaeme about Felker and his mage, they were turned aside. Jaeme appeared to be completely under Felker's thrall and would not listen to either one of them.

Their shared distrust had drawn the two of them together, a heady experience which Dec was enjoying to the fullest. It was the closest he had ever been to a woman so intelligent and yet so beautiful. Felker was lavishing their young lord with unctuous praise and outlandish compliments, fawning on his every word. It was a thoroughly shameless display of shallow flattery, and neither Laela nor Dec could understand how Jaeme could be taken in so completely.

On the morning of the third day, the great force set out in trepidition, following the path indicated by Andrew. But no sign of the orcs had been found. Indeed, the thought had crossed more than a few minds that perhaps Andrew had exaggerated the whole thing. Then the wind shifted and carried the scent of Fierdras to them.

"There's death in the air," said Jaeme, softly sniffing the breeze.

"Aye, 'tis a foul stench," replied Felker, still at Jaeme's side. The horses caught the scent, too, and became restless. Scouts sent ahead came running back and stopped short before their lords.

"It's all burned to the ground!" one of them exclaimed, out of breath.

"And what of the orcs?" asked Felker quickly.

''None remain save rotting corpses, m'lord,'' answered the other scout.

The two lords dismounted, as did the rest of the knights, and the group proceeded on foot.

They entered the desolate ruins in silence. There was nothing to be said; the terrible sights shriveled the words on their tongues. The charred remains of the dead were gently gathered and placed in a mass grave, the stone marker with the name of the town engraved upon it serving as the single headstone.

As the army marched out of Fierdras, along a course flanked by the ancient Offa's Wall, all were subdued, shaken, and grim. The air had changed. In the beginning, despite their mission and a tinge of fear, there had been a feeling of gaiety, a spirit of adventure. The blackened remains of Fierdras had changed all that. Now, they were focused and the focus was on death, theirs or the orcs. Nothing less would do.

Chapter 12
HUNTERS

WHATEVER THE REASON, THE ORCS HAD MADE LITTLE IF ANY attempt to conceal their trail upon leaving Fierdras. At first, scouts had gone out in all directions, but there was only one trail to follow. Perhaps they had been in their cups or perhaps they had simply not cared whether they were followed or not, confident of their own power. The way led at length away from the wall and north toward the Pictish Wastes.

"No doubt that's where they come from," commented Jaeme as he discussed the change in direction with Felker and the scouts.

"And to which they shall return in safety unless we pick up the pace," said Felker anxiously. They rode on. The trail, strewn with bits and pieces of the lives of those the orcs had slain—a petticoat hung up on a bush, a pewter cup smashed flat, a straw hat with the crown punched out—was an invitation, a rude insult which the pursuers could not ignore.

It was this that troubled Laela. She had no love for orcs or respect for their intelligence, but they were known to be cunning and sly and she could not imagine that they would be so foolish as to leave this broad trail . . . unless they wanted to be followed. She again rode ahead and tried to convey her worries to Jaeme, but Felker, who remained at all times by the side of the young earl, ridiculed her and made her look foolish. Jaeme was disturbed by Felker's attack on Laela, but before he could say anything, the slimy fellow pointed out a bit of cloth hanging from a rock and set out at a gallop. Jaeme's horse followed nose to tail. The Druidess gave up and returned to her place alongside Dec.

No one was able to get close to Jaeme without Felker's listening in on the conversation and somehow twisting things around so that nothing came out the way they had intended.

"Gratten must have Jaeme under a spell of some sort," Laela theorized to Dec as they rode along. "Could you not detect this and find a way to break or counter it?" Her deep green eyes caught his and he could not refuse.

"I'll give it a try," Dec answered with a note of despair in his voice. "I've never been very good at detecting things unseen. Sometimes I wonder if the magic lies in Felker's clever tongue." He grinned across at Laela. "I would very much like to silence that wagging thing." Dec dug into his bag and thumbed through a small worn leather tome, mumbling to himself. After a few minutes he let out a little exclamation, winked at Laela, nudged his mount to a trot, and rode toward the head of the advancing column.

Some time later he returned, a dejected look on his face. "I rode next to Gratten as long as I could stand it, making idle talk, then by the side of the Lord of Elfwood. But my bit of magic could descry nothing unusual." He paused. "Then, of course, my magic may not have worked at all. The only proof comes with detection."

"Or it may be as you said earlier," offered Laela. "Jaeme is under the thrall of Felker."

The ground underfoot was changing from grassland to marshy bogs, and the long stream of people, knights, lords, footmen, servants, pack animals, and wagons which made up the pursuing force began to snake back and forth in the absence of solid ground. The Pictish Wastes were a nasty bit of geography—swamps, quicksand, shifting sand dunes, and morasses that could swallow a horse with no difficulty. The lands were home to the orcs and many other hideous creatures. It was also the perfect place for an ambush.

The scouts returned with the news that the orcs had split in two. The smaller of the two groups was headed directly north into the worst of the Wastes. The main body had turned south, back toward Offa's Wall and civilization.

A hasty conference was held. "These orcs are up to no good," Jaeme said, stroking his smooth, beardless chin with his fingertips. "Even though it bothers me that some might escape us, perhaps it would be wisest if we did not fall into their trap and permit ourselves to be separated. Perhaps it would be best to let the northern faction go. We would be at a disadvantage in the Wastes, and they can do no harm there. Thus, we could ride with all speed after the larger group and stop them before they harm any more villages."

"A wise plan, m'lord," Felker said smoothly, attempting to position his horse so that it came between Jaeme and Laela and Dec. "But dare we take the chance that this is but another cunning and devious plan? Supposing that after we leave they circle around behind us, march out of the Wastes, and fall upon some other village, such as Merton, which lies just beyond the horizon."

Dec circled nearer Jaeme. The young mage had a pensive, obsessed look on his face, as though concentrating very deeply on something. Not by accident, he came too near, and jostled the young lord in his saddle.

"Oops, sorry!"

Jaeme turned to chastise Dec, but suddenly a feeling of relief flowed through his body. A weight had been lifted from his mind. He tugged at his lower lip and turned back to Felker. "Yes, I suppose that is a possibility," he said with a frown. "But I am unfamiliar with the Wastes and know them only from their fearsome reputation. I—"

"Fear not, m'lord," Felker interjected, although Jaeme had said nothing about being afraid. "I know the Wastes well. I have hunted in them since I was knee-high to a cockleburr," he went on, insinuating that even a child could find his way among them. Jaeme flushed darkly.

Felker, amused by his own words, sharing the laugh at Jaeme's expense with his men, pretended not to notice.

"My men and I will follow the northern group, m'lord. But do not be alarmed. I will take only a third of them, leaving you with a force large enough to deal with the rest of the orcs."

The words could easily be interpreted as an insult, but Felker's face was open and guileless, showing no sign of an ulterior motive. Yet ever since Dec had bumped into him, the sway that the man had held over Jaeme seemed to be gone, and the young Earl of Elfwood saw Felker in his true colors. He thought to remind the man that he was in charge of the expedition and it was therefore his place to direct the strategy. But here was Felker, smiling at him, waiting for his decision.

Jaeme looked away, uncertain. It seemed such a petty thing to quibble about when the man had showed up unasked and volunteered himself and all his forces, placing them at Jaeme's disposal. Felker had never been one of

Jaeme's favorites, but he had to admit that none of the other lords had offered their services. But neither had he asked them.

"M'lord," Felker prompted.

"All right, we will do as you suggest," Jaeme said, feeling a twinge of alarm course through him, as though his body knew something that he did not. "But I want you to know," he added quickly as Felker began to turn his horse aside, "that I am NOT afraid to go into the Wastes. You misunderstood what I was saying."

"Of course, m'lord, of course," Felker said in a placating tone such as one might use to a quarrelsome child. Jaeme felt his face flush once again and he kneed his horse, a bit too hard, causing it to leap forward as he fought to keep sharp words from leaving his lips.

Diplomacy, or rather the lack of it, had always been the most difficult part of his training. Polonius often despaired that Jaeme would ever become a great statesman if he did not learn to keep a leash on his tongue. If Felker was any example of the mastery of the art of statecraft, Jaeme doubted he wanted to become a great statesman.

Nodding brusquely, Jaeme took leave of the still-smirking Felker. Orders were passed down the line and the great force split into two parts. One, under Jaeme, marched southwest along the still clearly visible trail. The other, under Felker, trailed off to the north, ever deeper into the Wastes. Felker had been true to his word and had sent fully two-thirds of his army with Jaeme, thus giving him a clearly superior force with which to face the enemy.

Lewtt, who was once again in good spirits, proved invaluable, and flitted back and forth during the course of the day reporting to his mistress on the whereabouts and the actions of the orcs. It was obvious that the orcs had plundered the alehouse thoroughly before torching it. Jaeme and his men found numerous empty ale pots and rum bottles littering the wake of the orcs' trail. There had been none before the two groups split up, Jaeme could only suppose that this group had concealed the booty from their companions. Soon, the men began to find individual trails wandering off from the main body, as orcs staggered about aimlessly, then rejoined the group. It seemed that the orcs were imbibing heavily. Good, it would only make their task easier.

The column came to a sudden halt. A single orc was found snoring in the middle of a lea by the path, arms and legs outstretched, dressed in various bits of woman's garb, some of them stained with blood. Its piggish snout was hanging loose, spittle and alcoholic fumes spilling out with the rumbling emissions. Jaeme dismounted and dispatched the foul creature with no mercy. "Get those clothes off the thing!" he commanded. Skyler stripped the garments from its filthy body, which was left to rot where it had fallen. They continued on.

Lewtt returned from yet another one of his flights, his little body trembling with excitement. It seemed that the orcs had become unable to travel any further, the drinking they had done preventing the coordinated function of their legs. They had set up a rude camp just over the next hill.

Jaeme lost no time in directing his men to surround the encampment while he himself scouted out the lay of the land and decided upon a course of action.

Creeping to the top of the hill, he looked down into a small vale, a cuplike valley surrounded on all sides by a circle of low hills fringed with trees that provided shelter as well as firewood. It was a perfect camp except for the fact that there was no water.

The orcs made no attempt at erecting tents or setting fires to cook a meal, only fell to the ground and began drinking in earnest and fighting among themselves as the number of jugs diminished.

Several of the men were anxious to set upon the orcs then and there, eager to retaliate for the destruction of Fierdras, as many of them had had friends and relatives among the victims. But Jaeme was of a mind to wait. It was only mid-afternoon and the sun high overhead. His army was large and sober; the orcs numbers were smaller and they were drunk. But most of them were still awake and quarrelsome. Orcs were nasty opponents and he doubted that drink improved their temperament.

"We shall wait until later, dark if need be, when hopefully the majority of the enemy will have fallen victim to their own overindulgence," he said softly, peering over a low hill at the orc camp. "At which time, our mage, Decutonius, can work his wiles." He turned to Dec, who stood behind with a stunned expression on his face.

"My-my wiles?"

"You did me a good turn earlier today." Jaeme smiled knowingly. "I'll warrant you can think of a way to wipe the orcs out in one fell swoop." He brought his hands together in a silent clap. "Crash! Boom! And we will not suffer a single casualty."

There was some grumbling among the ranks, especially among Felker's men, but Jaeme ignored it, knowing that he was right. Quietly, the army began to surround the orc camp.

All afternoon Dec mumbled and muttered to himself and made strange gestures in the air. Laela tried to speak with him, to see if she could be of any assistance, but he snapped at her peevishly, then apologized, running his fingers through his hair till it stood on end and made him look like a blond porcupine. Laela giggled and took her leave, which seemed to unnerve him even further.

He fumbled through the contents of his bag and racked his brain over and over for just the right spell. This would be his first test. This was real, the stakes were high. If he made a mistake, he could get them all killed . . . or even worse, kill them all. He did not want to make a mistake.

Over the course of the afternoon he thought of and then rejected a flood-spell (no natural source and no assurance that the orcs would drown. Besides, all that water might merely wake them up and make them mad), a charm-spell (what earthly good were two hundred charmed orcs?), and a forever-sleep spell. This had appealed to him for the longest time, but then he thought better of it; if it worked, there would be two hundred orcs littering the countryside, snoring loudly, scaring sheep and cows, and rendering a beautiful valley permanently unfit for human habitation. He finally settled upon his old favorite, the standby that had gotten him into so much trouble over the years, the good old fireball-spell.

He had wanted to be more creative, do something absolutely breathtaking that would really impress Jaeme and uh, Laela, but he finally came to the conclusion that getting the job done and done right with no mistakes would be the wisest thing to do. There was virtually no chance of his making a mistake with the fireball; he knew it backward and forward and had all the necessary components on hand.

The decision made, he had only to wait until Jaeme commanded, hopefully at sunset or after dark. He smiled, knowing that the fireball would look its most spectacular after dark. As night fell and the valley blended into total darkness, Dec was delighted to see that there was no moon, nor had any of the orcs revived long enough to build a fire. All to the good, for light, any light, would only reduce the effect of the fireball.

He was ready; there was nothing more he could do to prepare himself. Jaeme had given him the go-ahead. The men were all in position, a thin line of them to the west, south, and east. The main numbers were concentrated atop the hill to the north, for that was the direction it was judged that the survivors would flee after the fireball landed in their midst. Jaeme and his friend Joseph stood behind the mage, with Laela alongside him, Lewtt perched in her hair.

Perhaps it was her scent, that disturbing elusive fragrance that hung about her like musk, or maybe it was just the nearness of her that did it, causing Dec to concentrate just a little bit less than he should have. He so wanted her to have a good impression of him, think of him seriously, as an equal, that maybe his gestures were a bit too broad, too dramatic.

Whatever the reason, the fireball, an immense, brilliant ball of white-hot flame, was off-course as soon as it materialized, shooting through the dark night and landing with a terrific resounding boom just below the crest of the northernmost hill, just below the position held by their own men!

As the fireball thudded into the earth, it touched off an enormous crashing boom that washed back and forth across the vale bringing the orcs to their feet. Indeed it was so loud, Dec would not have been surprised had it wakened the dead! Hmmm, he thought to himself briefly, now that was a spell he had never tried.

The fireball had clearly illuminated the vastly superior force standing atop the hill waiting for the orcs to make their move. Unfortunately, it had also set the woods afire, as it had landed squarely in their midst. Even if the orcs had been suicidal and determined to fling themselves uphill and attack the army that so clearly outnumbered them, they would have had to fight their way through the blazing trees to do so, and not even orcs were that stupid.

Instead, they did the most logical thing—they retreated, turning en masse, running straight back the way they had come, straight back toward Jaeme, Joseph, Dec and Laela and Lewtt, and a handful of clearly terrified soldiers. Some of them, a group from Harrowhall, dropped their weapons and ran for their lives. Dec could scarcely blame them; he wanted to do exactly that himself. Who knows? he might have done so had it not been for Laela, for he was already feeling the effects of the spell, becoming woozy and lightheaded and weak in the knees. He didn't even know if he had it in him to try it again.

Only the fact that there was really nowhere to run and that Laela had turned to him and was looking at him with those incredible green eyes, caused him to stand his ground and try again.

Jaeme drew his sword, saying, "Decutonius, they're almost on us. Do you have another one of those in you? If not, I strongly suggest that you and Laela get behind us now." Joseph and the others drew their swords and stepped forward, prepared to meet the advancing horde of terrified orcs.

"I can do it again. But I fear that is you who had better back away. It's going to be close!" This time Dec was more than a little careful, shutting his mind to thoughts of Laela and her disturbing scent, trying to shut out the vision of two hundred screaming orcs heading straight for him with swords and pikes pointing the way. His stomach contracted, already imagining the sharp blades penetrating the soft flesh. But he persevered, and as the last words left his lips, his fingers traced the course in the air, and he added a prayer for good measure.

They were so close that the force of the blast knocked them off their feet. Dec lay on the cold ground for a moment, stunned. Then sensation began to come back to him. He was quite warm on one side and cold on the other. He raised a hand to his head, groggily, and felt his eyebrows frizzle and break off beneath his fingers. His head ached. He tried to touch his head and came away with a coarse, crispy chunk of what felt like cooked sponge but stank like burned chicken feathers. He blinked, trying to see what it was. His eyes hurt. Suddenly, he became aware of the pain. His whole face hurt, his nose, his cheeks—ow—even his lips! What was the matter? Had he missed again and blown himself up? He struggled to rise, to see, but fell back, too weak and in too much pain to even get to his feet. He lay there on his back and looked up at the dark sky through narrowly slitted eyes, wondering if this was the end of his inglorious career, if he were about to be turned into orc pie. He wondered what had become of the others, Laela, her little sprite, Jaeme. He hoped that they were all right, that he had not killed them. He was awash in misery at the thought of his failure. He had let them down, he had let them all down, he . . . His pathetic self-pitying was abruptly interrupted by numerous hands which grabbed hold of him and flung him into the air. Well, this was the end. He wished he could bid his parents farewell, he wished . . . Wait, what was this? Singing? Huzzahs? Dec listened more carefully through ringing ears, and managed to catch every other word or so. So many voices were speaking that he was finally able to make some sense of what they were saying.

He had succeeded! He had not failed after all! His

fireball, bigger and even more powerful than the first, had landed directly over the heads of the tightly bunched band of orcs, felling them like lightning-struck trees! Those that were not immediately killed by the withering heat had been swiftly dispatched by the army which had flowed down into the glade and slaughtered every last survivor. And he, Decutonius Consulus, was once again a hero!

Unfortunately, Dec was barely able to take part in the victory celebration, although he did his best to enjoy it vicariously. He had been a little too close to the blast, and a finger of flame had shot out of the center of the ball of fire and zapped him severely. Had he been even six inches closer, he would have been lying among the orcish ashes himself rather than having his health and long life toasted. As it was, he looked as though he had lain out in the sun for several days, somewhat like a roasted pig or maybe a pumpkin. His face was round and swollen and bright red, and his eyebrows and most of his hair was gone, fried to a crisp. The front of his clothing had been badly charred, and as the soldiers lifted him on high and threw him into the air, it fell away, leaving him naked to discover that the burn covered the entire front of his body as well.

Someone brought up a torch, and when his condition was discovered, he was gently draped in a blanket (which was wool and itched and chafed on his burns), and the soldiers were really very nice about not laughing. At least in his presence. All around him there was smothered snickers and guffaws disguised as throat clearing. But he was not fooled. He was the only fool. Would he EVER get it right?

Then Laela knelt over him. Her hair was somewhat singed, too. ''Take this ointment, you brave fool.'' She handed him a small horn of some pungent healing ointment.

"You rub it on like this." She dabbed some on his face and it brought instant ease. Her ministrations managed to make him feel a little bit better about himself. She had held his hand briefly, with never a mention of his poor aim. His appreciation of her grew even stronger.

"Thank you," Dec managed to whisper hoarsely.

Jaeme stopped by as well to pay his respects, then saw to the stacking of the bodies. He had ordered that they be searched in case there were any valuables belonging to the people of Fierdras. Along with the recovered goods his men found an unexpected and ominous item—a crumpled tunic, black, with a blaze of yellow in the center.

This startling find had so stunned the earl that he scarcely seemed to notice that anything was amiss with his mage, who was lying flat upon the ground wrapped in a blanket. Jaeme pondered the signifigance of the tunic as he paced back and forth beside Dec. Finally, receiving no useful input from the young mage, who was still reeling from the effect of throwing two spells in a row, he strode off, muttering to himself.

The vale stank of burnt pork, and after the initial celebration was done with, the army moved away from the scene of the battle, leaving the carnage to the foxes and crows and other scavengers. They set up camp a short distance away, upwind, although there was very little sleep for anyone that night.

In the morning, all were anxious to be on their way. The empty stretches of land were somehow unnerving, and now that the battle was over, they were seeing orc stragglers behind every twitching bit of foliage, though none were really there. Many an innocent bush met its doom that day.

There was great relief when, late that afternoon, a hail in

the distance announced the arrival of Felker and his band of men. Camp was made on the spot, for a small stream passed through the valley and all were tired. Round the evening fires, they exchanged the details of their separate victories.

"We chased them on horseback into a narrow glade," Felker said, "and you were right, they were lying in wait to ambush us." Felker stopped to sip at a mug of beer. "There was nothing for it but to fight for our lives. No room for magic, too close quarters." Gratten grumbled incoherently at his side, discontent obvious in his eyes.

"A bit of hot work, then," offered Jaeme.

"Aye, that it was." For once Felker seemed sincere, even to Dec, although his perception was probably altered by his burnt condition. Felker continued. "Once combat was joined, it was as vicious and dirty a battle as any I've ever experienced."

In the end, the orcs had been defeated, although several had escaped, disappearing into a swamp. A swamp that had swallowed up three of his own men who attempted to follow. They had suffered numerous other casualties as well, several deaths and serious injuries.

Gratten seemed to view Dec's part in Jaeme's victory as a personal insult, even though Dec was quite modest and retiring about his share in the glory. Thanks to Laela's salve, he was fit enough to walk and sit among the others. He'd have to get the formula for that stuff. In a single day it had repaired most of the damage he had inflicted upon himself. Dec supposed he should be more gracious, but Gratten annoyed him—no, it was more than that; he really disliked the mage and had no desire to make him feel better.

"Don't worry, old fellow," Dec said at last, in a patronizing manner. "I'm sure you would have done a fine job.'' His tone left little doubt in Gratten's mind that Dec meant nothing of the sort. Dec wondered if he'd gone too far, for suddenly the Red Mage's face turned dark and hard. Wisely Dec rose and smiled, then strolled off, whistling a happy tune.

Chapter 13

A DWEOMIC CONFRONTATION

ALTHOUGH IT HAD BEEN DECIDED THAT THE TWO ARMIES WOULD camp for the night, Jaeme was of a mind to ride on ahead with his mounted knights and return to Elfwood immediately. It worried him to be away, but Felker suggested that he would consider it an honor and a privilege to spend time with his new liege lord. Although Jaeme was never certain of how Felker accomplished it, the older man made him feel that he would be small and mean if he did not agree to share his time.

"See how the men appear to be enjoying the to and fro between the armies of Elfwood and Harrowhall," Felker said happily. "It is good that we get on so well." In fact, the encampment was almost festive, the men releasing the pent-up fears and nervousness which they had been unable to express before the successful conclusion of the encounter. Now, they were passing jugs of their own back and forth, and tales of their recent prowess were growing in boastfulness with each telling.

"Perhaps it will do the men good to celebrate these

victories,'' Jaeme commented dourly, ''If events continue as they have, happy times will be few and far between.''

''It would do you good as well.'' Felker proffered a mug of beer. Jaeme accepted and shrugged. He would stay. The most it would cost him was time. Surely it could do no harm. He raised the mug in a toast. Felker smiled.

The only ones who did not share Felker's joy were Dec and Gratten. Laela was not thrilled with the accommodations, surrounded by hundreds of drunken, beer-guzzling, belching buffoons, but she and Lewtt could easily remove themselves from the camp and wander the surrounding lands. Which is what they did.

Dec had no such options, for Laela and Lewtt had not invited him to accompany them and he had no desire to wander the wilds by himself. He had little in common with the soldiers and no desire to drink himself silly; he still had a headache from the fireballs. He walked aimlessly around the camp, whistling now to himself, taking in the sights. Jaeme and his close friends were busy drinking with Felker and a group of his henchmen. He then caught sight of Gratten, sitting off by himself next to a fire.

The inexplicable dislike Dec felt for Gratten had grown rather than diminished. The mere mention of the Red Mage's name was enough to enrage him. He turned away and stalked around the camp, looking for things to occupy his time, but there was really nothing he could do and eventually he found himself back at Gratten's campfire, sitting across from the Red Mage glowering at him. Gratten, in turn, glowered just as fiercely back at him.

For a time, they contented themselves with dirty looks and muttered asides. But as a moon came out and shone down upon the two, the silent enmity heightened.

It began simply enough. Gratten turned aside for a

moment and Dec succumbed to a fit of childishness, discreetly tipping Gratten's mug over into the dirt with a small stick, spilling his drink. The Red Mage did not appear to notice that the accident might not have been an accident, but soon after, Dec discovered that the sprinkling of coarse ground pepper he had applied to his roasted quail had somehow mysteriously turned to flavorless bits of dirt.

Pretending to fan the quail with his hands, declaring it too hot to eat, Dec motioned furtively, and Gratten's boiled new potatoes jumped out of the pot and into the fire. Dec expressed sympathy and complained about the inattention of the camp cooks.

Rising, ostensibly to crush the line of biting ants that had suddenly found a strong interest in his shins, Gratten brushed his robes and legs, rather extravagant brushings Dec thought as he suddenly found his throat closing around the bit of bread he had just swallowed. He tried to hack, to cough, to spit the offending chunk out, but nothing worked and soon he began to feel things growing dark around him, darkness punctuated with flashes of red. There was a loud roaring in his ears. Then, there was a great thunk on his back, which all but drove him face first into the ground. Again and again the blows came, and he drew a deep breath into his lungs, sputtering and gasping, the salvation almost more painful than the choking.

When he recovered, shaking and weak-kneed, he found Gratten smiling down at him, holding out a mug of hot tea. "Yew were coughing a bit. Thought yew might need a drink."

Dec's throat did hurt and he started to reach for the mug but then snatched his hand back, cursing himself for a fool. Who knew what was in that mug!

It would be nice to report that the two mages settled their

differences and acted like mature adults, highly trained professionals, instead of peevish, petty children. But alas, such was not the case. Instead, the exchange of magical mischief increased in magnitude, with each mage doing his best to subjugate and humiliate the other. They were no longer even bothering to conceal their gestures. Or their name-calling.

Gratten accused Decutonius outright of being a puffed-up, pimply faced adolescent nincompoop.

Dec responded by declaring Gratten to be an ancient, incontinent, senile old smellbag.

A tin plate whizzed past Dec's head, the buttered bread and haunch of quail following at a slightly slower rate, spattering Dec's robes with congealing gravy.

The mug of tea Gratten had offered upended itself over his head, plastering his thinning hair to his skull.

The commotion had attracted a large crowd of soldiers who stood around the mage's campfire, watching the exchange of hostilities with great interest. All manner of objects began flying through the air, assailing the waving, gesturing, wildly gesticulating wizards who shouted and cursed in incomprehensible tongues, all the while weaving and bobbing in an effort to avoid the spells and objects being flung by one another.

Rather than attempt to stop the fight, the soldiers began making bets on which mage would win. There was much discussion of the various strengths of each. Some liked Dec for his youth and his ability to think up strange and bizarre taunts. Gratten, on the other hand, had a large number of supporters who pointed out that his age would be the deciding factor, for he had learned how to flow with the spell and not let it exhaust him. His staying power was judged to be the greater.

Indeed, it seemed as though those who had placed their grotens on Gratten would be the winners, for it was clear that Dec was beginning to tire. His gestures were beginning to slow, and his voice had become less vibrant.

Now, the wagers were changing, the winner no longer in question. Now the issue was not who would win, but what would happen to the loser. Some bet that Gratten would settle for severely trouncing the younger man, humiliating him in front of the gathered throng. But Felker's men, those who had reason to know and fear the Red Mage, stated flatly that the contest would be young Dec's first and final competition.

Who knows what might have happened had they been left to their own devices? But that was not to be. Lewtt, attracted by all the fuss and commotion, had flitted back into camp. He watched what was happening for a while. The sprite was basically indifferent as to the outcome of the dueling mages, but he remembered the warm feelings his mistress had felt for the boy.

Come quickly, mistress, he called to Laela.

She awoke from a half-sleep under a tree, some distance away in the wood. "What? Lewtt, what's wrong?" A mental picture of Dec's predicament appeared in her mind.

This Decutonius fellow is not long for this world without your help, Lewtt answered. He needn't have said anything, for Laela was already hurrying through the darkness to see what she could do.

Lewtt hovered above the fire that separated the mages, urging his mistress to speed upon her way, for it was clear that the end was near. Lewtt had his little tricks he could pull, but there was nothing he could do to help now. Dec had tripped over one of the many objects that littered the ground and was lying there, dazed.

Gratten rose to his feet and leaped slowly over the fire as though he were frozen in time. Some of Felker's men cheered. The Red Mage loomed above his fallen opponent, gesturing, drawing the moves out slowly, confident that he could not lose. He drew back his stiffened fingers, ready to deliver the *coup de grâce,* when suddenly, his robes flew up over his head and wrapped themselves tightly around his upper body, much as a washerwoman would wring out a wet garment, twisting tightly until all the moisture was squeezed out.

Dec had raised a hand and brushed it across his forehead, attempting to clear the cobwebs from his mind when Gratten's robes flew upward. Those of the soldiers who had backed Dec and had been groaning about their impending loss, were now screaming ecstatically, pounding each other on the back and jeering at the Red Mage's supporters.

Dec himself was astounded at the sight which met his somewhat blurred vision. Had he done that? He supposed so, but how? Things had gotten a bit muzzy there for a minute and he didn't really remember doing any such thing. As a matter of fact, as Gratten's robes twisted tighter and tighter, squeezing the mage like a lemon, his muffled cries scarcely audible, he could not figure out for the life of him how or what was going on. It obviously wasn't his doing.

"Wave your hands!" whispered a female voice. "Do something! Help me out here!" The hushed directive, delivered so close as to leave his ear warm, startled Dec as much as the robe trick. The scent of Laela struck home. Fortunately, he did not give himself away, turning the wide-eyed look into part of a violent, scary expression. He struggled to his feet and skipped and danced around the hapless Gratten, making it seem as though he were indeed responsible for the mage's demise. Suddenly the Red Mage tumbled backward into the fire with a howl.

Dec turned triumphantly to the crowd of onlookers, which now included Jaeme and Felker. "You better throw some water on that old windbag before he burns up!" He turned his back and marched away from the fight on his wobbly legs. Several men rushed forward and rolled the defeated mage in the dirt, putting out his now-burning robe.

Later that night, when order had finally been imposed by Felker and Jaeme, and the two mages separated by the length of the camp, Dec crawled humbly over to where Laela sat scowling under a tree.

"Thank you for what you did," he said softly. "That invisible trick was really great. You'll have to teach it to me. I think he might have killed me if you hadn't stepped in."

"You *think* he would have killed you?" The scorn dripped off Laela's tongue. Gad! Were all humans this stupid? How had the boy managed to stay alive this long? He was a disaster waiting to happen.

"But I was doing pretty good there for a while," Dec said, not wanting to appear entirely helpless.

Laela shook her head in disgust, and sighed. "Because of you, I must spend the night in this rowdy camp lest Gratten sneak over and snuff you in your sleep."

Despite the knowledge that he had really lost to Gratten, Dec was pleased with the turn of events. To the Red Mage and all present—save Laela—it would be thought that he had won the confrontation. More important, it was beginning to look as if she actually liked him. "Ya know, Laela, a man could learn to love a woman like you," he said.

Laela merely muttered something incomprehensible, pulled a moleskin blanket over her head, and went to sleep.

In the morning, the two lords parted, each taking his own

army. During the night, it had somehow been decided, although once again Jaeme could not remember how and why it had happened, that Felker would remain in the area for a few days, patrolling the region, making certain that all of the orcs were well and truly gone. Jaeme and his forces would return to Elfwood.

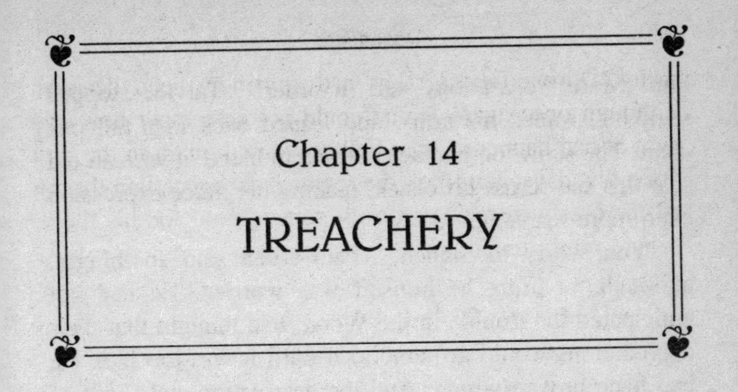

Chapter 14

TREACHERY

ELSEWHERE, PENWARDEN, LORD OF CAERPENH, WAS HAVING HIS own problems. Talvice, leader of the black-garbed Frankish mercenaries was unleashing his anger.

"Why did you not tell me that there was anything to watch for in the forest? You told me that we could expect to do our work without discovery or danger! Do you know how many men I lost? And those who survived are next to useless; their minds are addled. All they do is sit around and drool.

"It isn't like it used to be in the good old days, y'know. Good men are hard to come by. The men I lose cannot be replaced unless I personally go back to the continent. And now that isn't safe because young Elfwood has hired himself a mage and sent our ships back whence they came. We're trapped on this accursed island. This is costing me a fortune. And it's going to cost you two even more!

"It's not like we're getting anywhere, either, y'know," Talvice went on, snarling. "So we got rid of the old man. Hah! Now, we're saddled with the kid and he'll be on the watch, you can be sure of that. It won't be so easy to get to him! More 'reparations' are in order!'' Talvice stopped speaking, folded his arms, and leaned back in a tall oak chair. The scowl on his face seemed to blend in with an old scar that ran across his cheek, making his fierce expression even more fearsome.

''You worry too much,'' Penwarden said soothingly, although, in truth, he himself was worried. He had not anticipated the trouble in the Wood, had thought that their depredations would go unnoticed until it was too late. He had been proved wrong. And the destruction and flight of the Northmen was an even harder blow. No communications with the continent. Now he would have to do something to appease the irate Talvice, or lose his services, which was unthinkable.

''How much do you think these 'reparations' will cost?'' Penwarden asked quietly, although he himself thought that the word blackmail would have been appropriate. ''How much will it take to keep you content in the lovely land of Albion?''

Talvice mentioned a figure so high that Penwarden flinched. But he was well and firmly skewered; there was no way he could withdraw from the thing he and the others had set in motion. It had taken on an impetus of its own that was impossible to stop, even if he wanted to. Now he was but one branch of a many-armed juggernaut.

Penwarden hesitated for only a moment as Talvice rose and appeared to be on the verge of walking out the door. If he did that, it would cost even more to get him back. Hastily, he agreed to the deftly camouflaged extortion. Then, as Talvice relaxed, obviously pleased with the result of his demands, Penwarden continued.

''You realize, of course, that Felker has arranged it so that the castle is nearly deserted; it would be a perfect time to attack. If you strike quickly, you can take it with few casualties."

Talvice merely grunted in disbelief, and motioned to a servant who silently rushed over with a clay crock and poured the mercenary another large lager.

Penwarden spoke sharply, a hard edge to his words to remind the man that he was still in his employ. "Now is the time to strike, while the whelp is off chasing orc shadows and the castle is manned by only a skeleton force."

"You don't think your whelp will find the orcs?" Talvice asked, not the least bit perturbed by Penwarden's tone; he knew his own worth and it wasn't as though there were other armies of mercenaries just lounging around waiting to be called upon.

"I hope he does," Penwarden growled. "I'm counting on it. Felker knows what to do. He'll split away on his own and send the boy off to blunder into the main body of orcs. He's a fighter, yes, but not a leader. I can't see the boy winning out against them." Penwarden shuddered. "The orcs are unholy, larger in number than hoped for, and extremely overpaid. If luck is with us, Jaeme and his pitiful forces are mincemeat at this moment."

"I wouldn't count on luck," Talvice said dryly. "It has a way of turning sour when you least expect it. Especially with 'sure things.'"

Penwarden growled again. "That's enough talk of defeat. We will win or die in the attempt. Rouse your men and proceed to the castle with all speed. Do not come whining back to me about insufficient forces. An army of stuffed goats could take the place right now. I can allow a man one mistake, but never two. Do we understand each other?"

Talvice merely bowed, then placed his mug on the table and withdrew. As he marched down the corridor, shouting orders to his men, he mused about the manner in which Penwarden spoke to him. That was the problem with these men who hired him. All too often they forgot whose hand wielded the sword. Why should he, Talvice, be afraid of a fat, backward, small-time dandy like Penwarden? What did the man have to threaten him with? If he were militarily strong, he would have no reason to summon a mercenary army. No, if anyone were to "die in the attempt," it certainly would not be Talvice. In the meantime, the money was good, very good, and if what the fool said was correct, they could take the castle with few losses. And what did he care about losses? There was always more cannon fodder to be found. And if he did take the castle, there might be a sudden change of plans. A man his age . . . it was time to be thinking of his retirement. A large fief in Albion had its advantages.

Meanwhile, back at the castle, Polonius had entertained many of the same thoughts expressed by Penwarden. Felker's men had proved themselves to be diligent and seemingly reliable, standing guard at all hours of the day and night without complaint. He sent them on patrol to the far fields, and they obeyed Polonius' every command without question. They were abnormally compliant; he would have felt better if they had complained or been slow to obey an order. Something just didn't feel right.

Polonius spoke to the Elfwood Guard, one at a time so as not to attract attention, imparting to each his concerns. "We are outnumbered within our own walls. Be alert at all times. There is no shame in being defeated in war, but to be conquered at home by one's friends is the ultimate insult."

One night, several days after Jaeme had departed, there were odd happenings outside the castle walls. White lights were seen travelling from one side of the valley to the other, as though riders were carrying messages between two armies.

Signs of movement were glimpsed, but barely, as the night was extremely dark with no moon. Polonius could only make a guess as to what was going on. Finally, fearing that they were about to be attacked, he summoned two of his best men.

"The lights were seen moving in that direction, just behind those trees," the master-at-arms said, pointing out into the darkness from the top of the gate. "Travel silently, no swords or armour. And don't start any trouble if you find an enemy. I need information. Most of all, I want you two back alive."

"May we at least take our bows, sir?" asked one of the men. Polonius thought for a moment, then nodded.

"Bows and daggers, but again I caution you, don't use them unless you must."

The master-at-arms watched as a small door in the front gate opened. A dim shaft of light shone out onto the drawbridge. His two scouts came silently out and padded across the bridge. The door shut and the men disappeared into the blackness that surrounded them.

Throughout the long night, Polonius anxiously paced the ramparts, now and then clinging to the narrow stone apertures and searching the shadows, praying for their safe return.

Dawn appeared slowly that morn, timidly peeking through the heavy cloud cover one pale ray at a time as though uncertain whether or not to commit itself to full daylight. The master-at-arms gave up hope that his scouts would ever return. Weary, he began to descend the stair. He needed rest. A sudden shout from the high tower brought him back to the top of the gate. He squinted out at the field. Something was wrong. There were dark shadows on the grass. In the grey dawn that had replaced the night, Polonius' old heart faltered. Surrounding the castle was a circle of armed men, dressed in black tunics emblazoned with the yellow diamond.

The army made no move to advance, but merely stood with their weapons at the ready. Finally, Polonius tore himself away from the walls and raised the alarm. Men hurried to their posts, many of them struggling to don clothes, armour, and sollevets. No man cared to go to his death half-naked. The drawbridge rose, creaking, clanking, and complaining. At length the walls bristled with armed soldiers. Still the black army did not move.

Time stretched out as dawn yielded to full day, with the two armies facing off in silence. It was unnatural, and nerves were stretched to the breaking point. Polonius looked around and saw with satisfaction and surprise that Felker's men were standing fast at their posts, giving every impression of loyalty. Perhaps he had been wrong. Perhaps he had misjudged them.

Finally a rider approached the castle astride a broad-shouldered, dapple-grey horse and carrying a pole with a white flag attached to its tip.

''You there!'' He shouted. ''In the castle!''

Polonius strode through the waiting men and shouted down. ''Who are you and what do you want? Identify yourselves!''

''Who we are is of little concern to you,'' replied the rider, his deep voice easily heard even at that distance. ''We know of your weakened condition. Even now your lord lies dead in the field. As you can see, we outnumber you greatly.

What we want—nay, what we demand—is your full surrender.''

''I speak with no man who is afraid to state his name,'' hollered Polonius, somewhat taken aback by the remark about Jaeme lying dead. ''Hie yourself back to your master, whomsoever he might be, and tell him that Elfwood Castle does not treat with the nameless.''

They were brave words but, as Polonius knew, all too lacking in substance. Even if Felker's men remained loyal, the army outside the gates numbered three to four times those inside the walls, and he thought he had seen a siege engine or two, catapults, by the look of them, positioned near the village. Elfwood Castle was ill-prepared for war or siege and Polonius prayed that he could forestall a battle until Jaeme returned . . . if indeed, he still lived.

No sooner had he descended and begun to pass along what he had seen from his vantage point than a shout rang out from above. ''They got catapults, four of 'em!'' Polonius scarcely had time to digest the worrisome news before the men on the ramparts shouted warning of incoming fire.

And fire it was, flaming brands, dry brush soaked in oil, tied together round a rock and set afire as it was launched. The trajectory was perfect and balls of flaming brush began to fall out of the sky, raining down on everyone and everything inside the walls. Women and children ran about shrieking. Horses, pigs, cattle, and chickens vented their bowels as well as their fear. The thatched roofs of the animals' shelters and bales of hay caught fire as did several lean-tos and sheds. Time after time the catapaults were fired and soon the interior of the castle began to look like a scene out of purgatory.

Polonius did the best he could under the circumstances,

directing his own men to put out the fires. Thus, it was they who were caught out in the open by the deadly barrage of arrows that suddenly darkened the sky and rained down on the bailey. Many were killed instantly and many more badly wounded. Worse, many of the fires were still burning and billows of dark smoke rose in great clouds.

Polonius looked up, stunned. Why had there been no warning? He had not removed any of the men from the ramparts. They were Felker's men. Even as understanding came to him, the knowledge that Elfwood might indeed have been betrayed from within, a massive blow struck him in the chest, sending him to his knees. He gripped his left arm with his right, feeling the intense pain that spread through the muscles and out into his chest like white-hot fire. He looked down, attempting to see the wound, to see how bad it was and if it was mortal, although if the agony was any indicator, he would soon be dead.

But there was no arrow and no outward sign of injury. Polonius staggered to his feet, using the wall to pull himself up. It was his heart, that useless old bit of muscle that had betrayed him so many times in the past, although usually in battles of a different sort. He snorted as the pain washed over him again. He could not afford to die now; it simply wasn't possible. Richard, no—Jaeme needed him, the men needed him, Elfwood needed him to be strong.

Polonius never knew where he summoned the strength from, the strength needed to rise to his feet and survey the devastation that had befallen his beloved Elfwood. What he saw nearly brought him to his knees a second time. Most of those loyal to the castle were dead or dying, fires raged everywhere, and Felker's men still stood at the walls, untouched. They had known when to take cover, Polonius thought bitterly. He had not been wrong about them. It was small consolation.

Even as he took stock of the desperate situation, there were sounds of metal clashing, screams, and then the heavy groan of the gates swinging open, the clattering chain of the drawbridge being lowered, and the creak of the portullis as it was raised. Polonius stood helpless on the far side of the lower bailey and watched as black-clad horsemen riding four abreast charged in through the open gate. His head sank to his chest in shame. Castle Elfwood had fallen.

It wasn't that simple of course. There was more pain and humiliation yet to come. Polonius drew himself up as tall as he could, straightened his robes, and moved to the center of the courtyard to face the invaders.

As more black-garbed mercenaries thundered over the bridge, those inside circled around him, their faces hard and cruel. He kept his own face impassive, willing it not to betray the pain and grief as well as the hatred that beat inside his breast.

A rider pushed forward, his men opening their ranks to let him pass. There was more fear than respect in their eyes. "Earlier you would not treat with the nameless!" the man said, a thick accent making his words difficult to understand. "Well, I shall tell you my name. I am Talvice." He paused for effect. "Lord of Castle Elfwood."

Polonius winced at the words, then spat on the ground in answer.

"You would be Polonius, advisor to the young lord." Talvice chuckled. "You would have done well to have advised your charge not to have left his pretty castle. But then, if he had stayed, he too would likely be lying here dead, so who is to say?"

"What do you want?" Polonius demanded.

''There is nothing more that I want,'' Talvice replied. ''I already have it.''

''What do you intend to do with us?''

''That depends entirely on you,'' Talvice said, all amiability gone from his tone. ''I will spare the women and children, for now at least, if—and I urge you to think carefully before you answer—if I can trust you. I need your knowledge, old man, but I will not tolerate deception. One lie, one word to betray me, and they are dead. Are we clear on that point?'' Polonius could do nothing but nod his agreement. He could not ask the women and children to pay the price for his ancient ethics.

''Good,'' Talvice said, looking back over his shoulder. By now, black soldiers had filled the castle, lining the walls and towers, many standing side by side with Felker's men. Talvice said two words: ''Kill them!'' Polonius fought back the darkness that was threatening to close in on him. Had it all been some terrible joke? Had he not just agreed to do as the man asked!

But Talvice had not been referring to the women and children. It was Felker's men he had ordered killed. So unexpected was the command that it took them a moment before they realized what was happening. Too late, they fought back in an effort to save their lives, but it was hopeless; they too were outnumbered. There were screams of agony as the white-clad soldiers of Harrowhall perished and fell or were flung alive from the ramparts. Then the men on horseback rode down the few who tried to escape.

The cobblestones ran red with the blood of the dead. ''Why?'' Polonius asked as the pain grew in intensity and could no longer be ignored. He crumpled to the ground and stared up at Talvice who loomed above him. ''Why?''

Talvice shrugged as though the death of a hundred men

had meant no more to him than swatting a swarm of mosquitoes. "Why not?" he replied. "They betrayed you, their friends and neighbors, men they had lived and fought with, eaten and drunk with. If they could do such a thing to you, would they hesitate to betray me?" Polonius gave himself up to the darkness.

Chapter 15

THE MESSENGER

THE FUTURE LOOKED BLEAK. POLONIUS FRETTED AND PACED SLOWLY back and forth in his room, doing his best to ignore the persistent pain and weakness that plagued him. He knew in his heart that Jaeme lived, and he could not allow the young lord to walk into the trap that was waiting for him. Also, he suspected that Talvice would use him, display him prominently when the army returned, to show that everything was all right. Polonius could not allow himself to be the means for Jaeme's betrayal.

Talvice had been keeping a close eye on him. Yet he did not seem to believe that he was a serious risk, and so there were times when he was left unguarded. Such was the case this evening. Polonius opened his door a crack and peered into the dimly lit hall. It was empty. He held his keys in his hand to suppress their jangle and slipped silently out, not even shutting the latch behind him. He made his way through secret passages known only to a few, to the rooms of the young men in training to be knights. He walked quietly among the snoring lads till he came to Kirk, sleeping soundly, curled up on a bed of straw. Polonius shook the young fellow by the shoulder.

"What—?" The master-at-arms put his hand to the boy's mouth and his finger to his lips.

"Shh!" The boy recognized him and rubbed his sleepy eyes. "You must get dressed quickly," whispered the old man. Kirk did as he was told, and in a moment rose to his feet after pulling on his leather boots. Polonius motioned for the boy to follow him out through a low door in the side wall. Kirk eyed it in amazement as he went through, for he had never seen it before. Polonius pushed the door shut. They were alone in a cold narrow passage illuminated by single torch stuck in a cresset above them.

"I've been watching you, young man, ever since you came to us." Polonius began. "You have shown great spirit and intelligence. Your ordeal has proved your courage." Polonius laid his hand on the boy's shoulder. Kirk began to wonder what this was all about.

"You must go north again, young sir, and find the Lord of Elfwood. Take him the vile news of our defeat and imprisonment, and warn him of what awaits. Tell him also of Felker's treachery, and since we cannot be sure of anyone's loyalty, make certain that you convey this message in the utmost privacy and only to Jaeme himself."

Kirk trembled with pride, overjoyed at being entrusted with so important a task. Then a frightened look came over his face, for he had no idea how he was going to get to the place that he had to go.

"Come now, lad, part of our path lies in the open, for these secret ways do not lead to the place where you must depart." Kirk did not understand what the old man was talking about, but followed him willingly down the dark passage and through another door that led them back into a dark castle hallway.

Polonius knew the grave responsibility he was asking the boy to shoulder, but with the stakes so high, none of them had a choice in the matter; they were all poised on the edge of a knife blade. Risk and danger stood on one side and certain death on the other.

When he felt that they were unobserved, he led Kirk down to the lower scullery, a bleak place where servants toiled scrubbing pots and pans and dumping chamber pots of night soil into the hole that led to the River Tyrell, which flowed adjacent to the wall. At this moment, the room was empty, for everyone, scullery maids included, had been herded into the upper stories where they could be more closely supervised.

Polonius, after lighting a taper, reached up to a high shelf and produced a bulging cloth sack. He handed it to the boy.

"You'll need this," he said as Kirk opened it and examined the contents by the candlelight. It was full of small loaves of bread and rounds of cheese, some apples, and a jug of water. "Use it sparingly and it will last you several days." The boy nodded and slung it over his shoulder. Polonius blew out the candle.

There was another staircase, leading further down into the depths of the dark earth. This stairs was concealed behind a tall cobwebbed rack of brooms and mops. Not even those who spent their days in this dreary place knew of its existence.

Polonius pulled the rack away from the wall and gestured for Kirk to precede him into the darkness. Kirk swallowed hard. Reluctant to show fear before this important man, he did as he was instructed, even though his heart was in his throat. Only when the rack was closed securely behind them, did Polonius re-light his taper, which did little to illuminate the steep, slime-covered steps that fell away into the uncertain gloom below. Careful footing was necessary to avoid plunging down the slippery passage. Kirk could feel moisture accumulating on his face and hands and smelled water as well. He could only guess that they were very near the level of the river.

At last they reached the bottom of the treacherous stairway. Polonius drew a bit of paper marked with faint lines out of his pocket and after a moment's hesitation, started off in one direction. The boy followed closely, only to bump into him when the old man suddenly stopped.

"No, no, that's not the way at all," Polonius muttered to himself and they headed off the opposite way.

As they walked slowly along the cold, wet stone floor, Kirk could see dark corridors branching off in all directions and, occasionally, massive doors with grated windows and heavy bars fitted into the walls.

"Sir?" he said, plucking up his courage. "What is this place?"

Polonius cleared his throat, trying to find the right words so as not to frighten the boy. "Well, it was built many, many years ago by the first of the lords of the castle and enlarged by those who came after. Foodstuffs have been stored here and it offers safety for the womenfolk in times of siege."

"Yes, sir. But, sir, what about those heavy barred doors?"

Polonius said truthfully, "It has also served as a gaol, a sort of prison for those who were held in disfavor by the Lords of Castle Elfwood."

"You mean a dungeon!" Kirk's eyes grew large at the

thought. His granny had told him scary tales about this dungeon.

Polonius grimaced at the word. "Yes, a dungeon, but as you can see, it has long been out of use." Kirk did not answer, but his eyes grew large every time they passed one of the barred doors.

"Treasures, too, are hidden down here. Locked away from sight for many a year. Yet this place also has another very important function. There are tunnels here that lead long and far under the ground, out to the surrounding country. These tunnels may be used as the means of escape in times of extreme danger."

"Like now," said Kirk, feeling the importance of his mission.

"Like now," agreed Polonius. At length they came to another large door secured with a rusty chain and a huge iron lock. He handed the boy the candle.

"Here, hold this for me, lad." Polonius drew a large key ring out of his pocket and after a lengthy search, produced a long, skinny key which he inserted in the lock. After much struggle, it turned with a protesting screech and the lock fell open. Polonius fed the links of the rusty chain through a series of iron loops and dropped it to the stone floor with a clatter. It took both of them to pull the heavy door open enough to admit Kirk's small figure. Waves of damp, dank air flowed out of the dark interior and Kirk was not anxious to set foot inside.

"As much as I regret it," Polonius told the boy, "I must take my leave of you. My absence above may well have been noted, but I doubt you have even been counted. I have taken a risk coming this far, but I wanted to see you on your way. I need not remind you that the fate of this castle and all of those in it depends on you, as well as the life of your lord. Now go in safety. I will pray for you."

Polonius handed the boy two more candles as a reserve, lit one for himself, gripped the boy's hand tightly for a moment, and then he was gone, leaving Kirk alone. The one lit taper in the boy's hand did little to hold back the ominous darkness that pressed in on all sides.

Kirk set off, reminding himself that great undertakings were begun by the taking of the first step. It was something his mother had often said, and for a moment he was overcome with grief at the thought of her. He had rebelled against her firm hand and her rules that had governed his young life, but at this instant he wished for nothing more than to have her back, even if it meant going to bed in his corner of the cottage with only bread and water for supper.

But it was not to be. It was for his mother that he was doing this, and for all the others. Kirk wiped his eyes and stood straighter, vowing to succeed, to honor their memory with this deed. Even if he was scared to death.

He walked slowly at first, fearfully ducking under each cobweb that reached down at him. He found an old wet stick on the floor, which he picked up and used to clear the webs before him. After some time, the passage began to slope up and the floor was no longer wet underfoot. He was glad of that, for his feet were cold and damp.

Suddenly Kirk stopped in his tracks and his heart leaped into his throat. Far ahead of him in the dark glowed two tiny red eyes. No sooner had he seen them than they winked out and vanished. The hair on the back of his neck bristled. Hot tallow dribbled down on his hand and he nearly dropped his taper. He looked at it sadly. It was nearly gone, and he had no idea how much farther he had to go, or what manner of creature was down here in the dark with him.

Kirk put the wick of the second taper to the burning stub. It quickly caught. He snuffed out the old one and stuffed the remaining bit in his pocket, hoping he would not have to use it again.

He summoned up his courage and started off again, keeping a sharp eye out for any more mysterious eyes in the dark. The walls in this part of the tunnel were no longer hewn out of stone. Now they were fitted cobblestones. Timbers held the roof above his head and the floor was dry and dusty. As he was looking down, he saw familiar footprints in the dirt.

"Rats! Kirk you are a fool." He puffed out his chest. "Imagine, the great Kirk ascared of rats."

The dusty corridor continued on, sloping gently upward, but never with a turn to the right or left for what seemed to be a mile by Kirk's reckoning, I'm way beyond the walls, now he thought. Was this tunnel ever going to end and come to the surface?

His second taper was nearly gone, and reluctantly, he stopped to light the last one.

"You better end soon, mister tunnel!" he threatened, having no desire to finish his journey in pitch darkness. Kirk had hardly taken two more steps when he found himself face to face with a large boulder, sitting squarely in his path. At first he was filled with panic. He was trapped, and there was no way to go but back! Closer examination, however, revealed, slits on either side of the rock that were filled with loose rock and debris. He wedged his candle into a crevice and began digging furiously. He needn't have bothered. Suddenly the boulder swung open under his weight, and he tumbled into the dirt. The deep blue light of early morning flooded welcomely around him. He hadn't even considered just pushing on the boulder. He climbed to his feet, put out his candle, pocketing what was left, and emerged from the tunnel. Once outside, he pushed the boulder and it swung to seal the aperture as easily as it had opened it. It must be cleverly balanced with a series of levers and weights, he thought, just like the drawbridge, which he considered a mechanical marvel.

Kirk found himself standing inside a dense wood bounded by a rocky escarpment. Had he not just emerged from the rock behind him, he would never have suspected the tunnel's presence, so cleverly was it concealed. He could also see the castle in the distance, and now he understood why the tunnel had travelled so far before surfacing. This wood was the first available cover that was likely to be safe in the event of war. An invading army would, no doubt, camp just out of arrow-shot of the walls.

Compared to his dark journey in the tunnel, it was but a simple matter to find his way to Offa's Wall, and an even simpler matter to follow it north, toward Fierdras and Jaeme.

Two days later, having seen nothing more dangerous along the way than a pair of skulking wolves, Kirk was met by the forward scouts of the returning army. Instructing them that he was an important messenger sent to Jaeme upon direct orders of Polonius, he was met with good-hearted laughter. Kirk persisted, and the scouts hesitated, but the boy's air was so serious that at last they let him pass.

The army had paused in its march south, and Jaeme was seated beneath a tree, munching sullenly on a crust of bread. He rose on seeing the boy, and bade servants bring him food and drink. The two sat to talk, and Jaeme's attention was riveted on the boy as he told the sad story of the infamy and deceit that had befallen his home. His face lost its color when Kirk told of the losses they had sustained and of the fate of Felker's own men, the ease with which the mercenary had condemned the latter to death.

Jaeme summoned Dec and Laela, giving the guard firm instructions that they were not to be disturbed by anyone.

Kirk repeated his tale and as he did so, was suddenly interrupted. Fist slammed into palm. "I should have listened to Polonius; he was right!" Jaeme said bitterly. "Think how many have died because I did not listen."

"You could not have known," Laela said gently. "Do not blame yourself. What is done, is done. The good earth has claimed them now and they are past suffering. Your duty is to the living now, not the dead."

"Wise words," Jaeme said, smiling wanly at the woodland beauty to let her know how much he appreciated her support.

"But what am I to do? Attack my own castle? We cannot just leave them there!"

"Yes, an attack!" exclaimed Dec, visibly disturbed by the news. "We have to do something!"

"If it's a fight they want, we'll give them a fight!" cried Jaeme, two bright red spots appearing in the center of his pale cheeks. "These men are only mercenaries; they won't be willing to fight to the death. The men of Elfwood will be fighting for home and family. They'll be victorious or die!"

"You're certainly correct on that point," said Laela, not too diplomatically. "And die they will if you rush into a headlong attack."

The fire suddenly faded and Jaeme's eyes became soft and sad. "You are right, as usual. That is precisely what I've been trying to avoid. That's why I set my mage upon the orcs."

"What you want is a manner of attack that would cost the least number of deaths," Laela continued. "Perhaps you could retrace young Kirk's footsteps and try to take them by surprise from within.''

Not to be outdone, Dec had a suggestion as well. ''I'll cast a mass spell and persuade the mercenaries to surrender!'' he exclaimed, waving an imperious finger in the air.

Laela looked at him, head to one side, her expression stern. ''Have you ever done such a thing?'' she asked.

Dec was taken aback by the doubting tone in her voice. ''Well . . . I . . .''

''Successfully,'' she added, heaping further insult.

Dec tried to bluster his way through, but at last was forced to reveal that he had never even heard of such a spell, successful or otherwise. ''But I just know I can find a way to do it!'' he said with great optimism, defending his proposal strongly. After much discussion, a decision was made to implement both plans at once. Now they needed to sort out the logistics. Who would go where and do what, and when . . .

Chapter 16

PRISONERS AND PLOTS

POLONIUS RETURNED UP THE DARK STAIRS TO THE CASTLE PROPER AS fast as his tired old legs would carry him, the pain in his chest now ever-present, a low, dull ache that made him yearn for the comfort of his bed, his feather pillows, and a good, strong hot toddy. He wondered if he would survive the ordeal, then spoke sternly to himself. He had no alternative. He had not lived this long, advised four generations of Mortimers, only to see the castle and the family taken down by base treachery. Not while he was alive! He shut the mop and broom rack behind him, poured himself a small glass from a bottle in the scullery, and then silently made his way to his room. It wasn't hot toddy, but it would do. As he lay back on his bed collapsing into a deep sleep, his drink fell from his fingers, unconsumed.

The next morning, after he had roused the boys who would one day be knights for their training, he spoke to them in quite tones, explaining Kirk's disappearance. They were proud to be let in on the secret, and prouder yet that one of their number had been chosen for such an important mission. Later that day, as they practiced mock battles on the upper bailey, whaling away at each other with wooden swords, Polonius thought he detected a new determination among this lot. If they survived the current ordeal, they would, to a man, make fine defenders of the land.

As the day wore on, Polonius felt sure that his actions of the previous night had passed unnoticed. A fact that gave him a moment of wry amusement. Perhaps no one took him as seriously as he himself did. Well, all the better.

But if he had not been missed, it was because Talvice had been busy. Very busy. All the bodies had been cleared away and either burned or buried. The dead of Elfwood were buried with ceremony, as Talvice was endeavoring to win over his captives. Polonius, however, was not at all pleased with other goings-on. The remaining men-at-arms of Elfwood were stripped of their uniforms and imprisoned in a large room just off the Great Hall, under heavy guard. Talvice's men donned the Elfwood uniforms and helms and now paced the ramparts and stood at ease where they could be clearly seen. The bright green Elfwood pennant still flew from the towers. On the surface, it appeared as though nothing had happened.

Even worse, was what was told to the women and children who were herded into the Great Hall. Polonius watched and listened as Talvice stood up on the dais and, speaking in his thick accent, made it perfectly clear that it was up to them whether or not they, and their men, lived.

"I want everything to look as it did before I arrived." Talvice spoke almost sweetly. "Smoke from the cooking fires should be visible from a distance. Children will play in the courtyard. Peasants will come and go through the gate." The mercenary put his hands on his hips and glowered at the crowd of frightened women and terrified children. "Cooperate with me and all will be well. Scheme against me, attempt to escape or cause mischief and there will be hideous deaths.'' The women shuddered as one. He waved them away. ''Now get about your business!''

Polonius listened carefully as the meeting broke up. Most of the women believed the hard mercenary. The master-at-arms had to agree that another conqueror in his position could easily have slain not just the men, but every living creature in the castle. It was a barbaric tradition, practiced more often on the continent than even in the roughest times in the history of Albion.

The next day Talvice delivered another speech to drive home his message. It was a straightforward bargain. As a mercenary, he appreciated the value of money. He wanted their cooperation and was willing to pay for it, with the best coin he knew, lives that were dear to them. Polonius was filled with despair at the man's cleverness. Not for a moment did he believe that Talvice would keep his word. Had he not slain Felker's men under similar circumstances?

Polonius stood on the wall and stared out at the little village. The peasants there were allowed to go about their business, tending animals, bringing in the hay, but none were allowed to leave the area. Talvice's men lurked in every shadow, like so many thugs ready to strike, ever watching.

''Ahh, Polonius, it is time we had a talk,'' Talvice said smoothly, appearing out of nowhere and gripping Polonius by the elbow. ''Please come with me.'' Steering him along the wall and into the heart of the castle, he took Polonius up a flight of stairs to Richard's own chambers, which Talvice had clearly taken as his own. There he personally poured the master-at-arms a goblet of Richard's finest wine, although he took none for himself.

Polonius thought about refusing the offering, but the wine

was Richard's not Talvice's, and his faltering heart needed all the help it could get. As he raised the glass to his lips, memories of the very day that shipment had been brought into the castle and stored away came to mind.

For a moment the two men stared at each other. Then Talvice sighed, shaking his head. "You know, old man, under other circumstances, we could be friends, you and I." He paused, giving Polonius the opportunity to speak, but Polonius just eyed him suspiciously and said nothing.

Talvice tried again. "Things are not always what they seem. You, above all, should know that. You think that I am but a common mercenary, a thief in the night who kills and steals for gain. But you are wrong. Would it surprise you to learn that I am here by direct order of King Edmund?"

Polonius was startled in spite of himself. "Edmund!" he blurted out without thinking. "What are you saying? How dare you foul the name of our good king, you Frankish dog."

Talvice ignored the insult. "Say what you will, it was your king sent me." He poured more wine into the old man's glass.

Polonius was flustered. "Why would Edmund have anything to do with . . . this?"

"I am not at liberty to say," Talvice responded easily, smoothing his broad mustaches with his fingertips to conceal the look of glee that twitched at his lips. So, the old man could be gotten to after all, he thought to himself. Then he assumed a serious expression and continued. "But you may be assured that it is true."

"But we are loyal subjects!" Polonius began to pace back and forth, extremely disturbed by Talvice's words. "What have we done to deserve such treatment?"

"Have you been so ill-treated?" asked Talvice, now

determined to win the old man to his side. He would have to convince this man to do his bidding willingly; it would be impossible to force him against his will.

"How can you ask such a thing?" cried Polonius. He staggered, clutching his chest, obviously distraught. The master-at-arm's face turned an unnatural shade of puce that even Talvice could not ignore. The mercenary moved to the old man's side and eased him into a reclining position on a chaise, then slowly refilled the goblet. Another sip and the old man's breathing and color improved.

"Tell me," he said, reaching out for Talvice with trembling fingers. "Tell me what it is that you are saying. Has Edmund . . . Why would he . . . ? I don't understand," Polonius said fretfully, now appearing to be what he was, a very old man. Had he been younger and stronger, he would have seen through Talvice in a second.

Talvice thought quickly. "I am not at liberty to divulge the king's plans, you understand," he oozed. "But I think that I can assure you when I say that the king has not lost faith in you and regards those of Elfwood among his most loyal subjects."

"Then why . . ."

Talvice placed a finger alongside his nose. "Again I am not at liberty to say," he repeated. "But think for a moment. I did request that you open your gates to us. It was your decision to take a battle stance. We did not begin the fight."

"Yes, but . . ." The sequence of events had quite faded from Polonius' memory. The wine was having its effect.

"Nor did you suffer serious casualties," Talvice continued, wondering just how far he could take the charade.

"There were many deaths," Polonius protested.

"Yes, but not among your men," Talvice pointed out. "Only among the traitors."

"Felker a traitor?" Polonius was clearly aghast. "I have never liked the man, never trusted him, but a traitor?"

"Did his men not betray your trust?" asked Talvice.

"Yes, but . . ."

"There are no *buts* about it, good sir," Talvice said gravely, improvising as he went. "The facts are there for those who choose to see them. Edmund has long had his suspicions about Felker and sent me to test his loyalty. He has clearly failed."

"But your tunics, the black with the yellow diamond." Polonius' eyes became sharp and focused, and Talvice knew that he was not out of the woods yet. "It was an army dressed in just such a uniform who killed my lord Richard and set fire to the Wood. How do you explain that?"

"I was received by Felker," Talvice said without hesitation, "as per Edmund's direction. While we were under his roof, a number of my men reported that their uniforms had disappeared. They were returned before I could investigate." He stared at the ceiling. "I wish now that I had pursued the matter."

"Felker said nothing to us of your presence," Polonius said.

"Would you if you were about to commit such a base act against your liege lord?" asked Talvice. Polonius could only admit that he would not.

"But why was it necessary to kill his men?"

"The proof of their treachery was in their actions," said Talvice. Now enjoying the game and already half believing his own words, he was beginning to work up a real rage against the dead men. "They pretended to be your allies but turned on your men and opened the gates to us. How could I do otherwise? Alive, they would have been like a poisoned arrow poised at our hearts, a constant threat. There was no way I could allow them to live. Surely you can see that?"

Polonius was confused. The man's words were hard to refute. Everything he said could be explained, but still, there was something about the whole affair that troubled him. Edmund was not a complicated man, despite the fact that he was king. If he had doubts of a man's honesty, he would fetch the man up on the carpet and question him in that royal roar of a voice and keep at the poor fellow until he had the truth of the matter. There were no devious tricks or plots in the king. It was not like him to go to such lengths to implicate a man in his own treachery. But people changed. Perhaps it had happened just the way Talvice said. Polonius' mind was almost a blur.

"What is it you wish of us?" he asked, and Talvice was overjoyed, although he took pains not to reveal any such emotion.

"I wish nothing more than your continued cooperation and goodwill," Talvice said expansively. "Do not reveal our presence to Felker and your lord when they return. We must take Felker unaware if we are to expose the full extent of his treachery and take him and his men prisoner with no needless loss of life."

Polonius said nothing, merely nodding although it was obvious that he was still troubled.

"If you will do this for me, none of your people will come to harm, and as soon as we have taken Felker and his men captive, I will release your men. Edmund himself will be grateful for your help."

"Why can you not release them now?" Polonius asked querulously.

"I would do so gladly," Talvice said earnestly, "but you know how hot-blooded these young fellows are. No matter how we explained it to them, one of them would find it necessary to put a knife in my back or start a fight with my men and then I'd be obliged to do something drastic. I think it best for all concerned that they remain confined in the castle for the time being. They'll be well fed and rested and ready to fight if Felker will not thrown down his arms willingly.

"What say you? Will you not accept my offer?" Talvice said in a winning manner. "I would rather that we were friends than enemies."

Polonius nodded slowly. Something was still not right. Oh, the words were correct, but there was a feel to the man that Polonius did not like, a feeling of wrongness. Polonius had learned much over the decades of service to his lords, diplomacy and the ways of the world, but when one came down to it, there was really no better method of weighing a man or a situation than one's own intuition. Polonius had learned from bitter experience that when he went against his intuition, he always regretted it. And this time his intuition told him that despite the smooth words, this Talvice was as crooked as a salamander in spring. Furthermore, he seemed to have some hidden agenda of his own. Whosoever's pay he was in had better watch his own back as well.

But Polonius had not wasted all those years of service; he had learned to play the game along with the best of them, and there was no purpose in revealing his plans to Talvice. Better to let him think that he had been convinced. Polonius winced. All this thinking was beginning to hurt. The mercenary took it as a request for more drink, and more wine flowed into the old man's goblet.

He shall think I am taken in by his clever words, Polonius reasoned to himself. Perhaps if I appear to be no more than a doddering old man on his last legs, he might inadvertently reveal some bit of his true plans. My job will be to watch and listen and stay alive until Jaeme's return. Then, and only then, can I be of any help.

"I agree." Polonius said aloud at long last.

Talvice's smile turned into a broad grin.

"What is your pleasure?" asked the man-at-arms in a feeble voice. Best to reinforce the notion that he was but a tired and helpless old man, which, he thought ruefully, was not too far afield from the way he truly felt.

"If you are up to it, perhaps you could show me more of the castle. I am much interested in its construction," said Talvice.

I'll bet you are, thought Polonius as he nodded his head and said aloud, "Certainly. There is much to see."

Later in the day, they toured the castle together. Polonius had fortified himself with several hours of needed sleep. Although his arm and chest still ached, he felt rested and better prepared to deal with the villain Talvice.

They toured the castle from the top of the ramparts down to the kitchens. Talvice seemed impressed with all that he saw, but when Polonius turned to climb the stairs that would take them back to the courtyard, Talvice spoke up rather sharply. "Haven't you forgotten something?"

"Eh?" asked Polonius, playing the part of a doddering old man to the hilt.

"The lower levels, I believe . . ." Talvice said, pulling a detailed diagram out of his sleeve. With a sinking heart, Polonius recognized it as being annotated in Richard's own tiny, cramped script. That could only mean that Talvice had found and gone through Richard's records and correspondence. "I wish to see the lower levels," Talvice repeated with a hint of steel in his voice.

"The lower levels?" Polonius quavered. "Whyever for? No one goes down there . . . dark, damp, unpleasant. No need to go down there. Can't even remember how to get there,'' he said in an addled voice, turning again and shuffling away.

''I believe it's right over here,'' Talvice said triumphantly, walking directly toward the unused broom rack. He grabbed hold and gave it a pull. It came open on rusty, protesting hinges.

''Oh, well, imagine that,'' Polonius said weakly, avoiding Talvice's eye. ''Still, no need to go down there, nothing to see.''

''Then I'll go myself,'' said. Talvice. He produced a handful of candles and a tinderstone. ''I want to see everything.'' Against his will, Polonius was forced to accompany him, hoping that no sign of his earlier passage remained visible.

''Here, let me go first,'' he said, pushing past Talvice, adding, as he hesitated at the top of the dark stair, ''It has been a long time, but as I recall, the way is full of unexpected turns.'' He stepped down before Talvice could protest.

He felt for each step, and using his age and infirmity as cover, wiped each step with his searching foot and in the doing erased any trace of his and Kirk's earlier visit. They reached the bottom of the steps in due course and Talvice looked at him suspiciously. ''There were no twists or turns in the stairs, old man!''

''Oh, well, it's been a long time,'' Polonius said quaveringly. ''I've forgotten more than I ever knew. I suppose I was thinking of some other steps.''

Talvice glared at him, but how was he to prove that Polonius was lying? Fortunately, he was more interested in seeing what lay beyond than in harassing the old man.

Candle in hand, he explored the dark reaches of the lower

levels, and if he saw the faint trails where Kirk and Polonius had walked, he gave no sign.

"Where are the devices of . . . persuasion?" he asked.

"We have no need for such foul things," Polonius said with heartfelt disgust. "My lords have never believed in the necessity of such avenues. They were all noble men!"

Talvice walked forward and came to a barred cell. He peered inside. "Well, some of your lords obviously were a little less noble than their descendants, or these accommodations would never have been built," Talvice replied with more than a hint of laughter in his voice.

"Neither my lord Richard nor his son would ever stoop to such methods," Polonius said stiffly. "Nor will I be party to such goings-on!"

"Fortunately for your gentle sensibilities, such decisions will never rest on your shoulders," Talvice said dryly. "More to the point, however, is the problem of these tunnels."

Polonius wavered on his feet. This was the last straw! With all the perspicuity of a hunting hound, Talvice had nosed out several of the concealed entrances, doorways to the tunnels that would eventually converge and rise in the distant wood. But he had shown no particular interest in them, and Polonius had dared to hope that he had failed to recognize their significance. He had been wrong; the mercenary was sharper than he had given him credit for. He would do well not to underestimate the man in the future.

"Where do they go?" Talvice asked. "They do not seem to be noted in the diagram. A curious omission, would you not agree?"

Polonius knew that they had been purposely left off the map, for he himself had drawn the diagram many years before when Richard's father had passed away. The tunnels had been left off for good reason. They were not intended to be found by anyone except those who had been informed of their existence, namely, trusted members of the inner family. Those who needed to ask where they were, or where they went, were the enemy. Still, he could not afford to antagonize Talvice.

"There are many secrets in an old building such as this one, sir," he said politely, neither answering nor enlightening the man. "Now, if there is nothing else you wish to see, perhaps we might go. This damp air makes my bones ache."

"Of course, after you," Talvice said with an extravagant bow. "Please lead on." Polonius climbed the stairs, resting frequently, wondering, by the man's tone and curious grin, if his earlier attempts at wiping the stairs had gone undetected after all.

Once they were back in the courtyard, Talvice lost no time in directing a squadron of his men down into the underground chambers with orders to search out any tunnels that he might have missed. Any they found were not to be left unguarded for a single heartbeat. Polonius felt his hopes shrivel at the alacrity with which Talvice was obeyed. His men hung on his every word and appeared to be completely loyal. It would be impossible for anyone to sneak back into the castle through the tunnels. Now he had need to warn Jaeme a second time!

Despite Talvice's promises, Polonius knew that his young lord was being lured back into a trap from which there would be no escape, and he himself, was part of the bait.

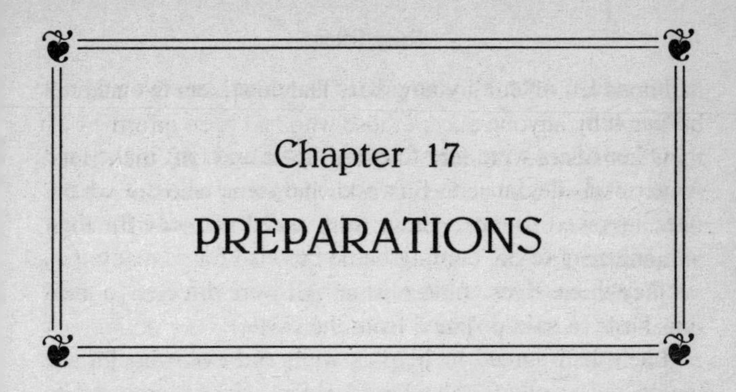

Chapter 17
PREPARATIONS

A FEW LEAGUES DISTANT, JAEME WAS DETERMINED NOT TO BE drawn into a trap and was doing his best to extricate himself from the situation. He called Joseph Willoughby to him.

"Not long ago," Jaeme began, "we were young lads drinking ourselves silly in Ahtska." Joseph smiled, putting his hand to his head in mock pain.

"Now I am Lord of Elfwood, and you are my most trusted knight."

"Things have indeed changed," said Joseph. "Though I'll not say for the better."

"Take what men you need, and ride round the countryside. I want you to gather as many men as possible. Hie to the villages and the towns. Bring this army to Elfwood as quickly as you can. I'm counting on you."

"It shall be done, m'lord." Joseph knelt before his lord.

"Cut that out!" exclaimed Jaeme, slapping his friend on the shoulder. Joseph stood, laughing. They shook hands quietly. Kirk, who had watched this strange exchange between friends, insisted on going along. Jaeme shrugged. "All right, young, man, but you must follow Joseph's every command.'' After all young Kirk had done, Jaeme could not refuse him.

Other riders were sent to every castle and lord in the land who owed allegiance to Elfwood, and some who did not but were avowed friends. These were asked not only for their commitment to the coming battle but also for as many men as they themselves could muster. All were directed to meet posthaste, a safe distance from the castle.

Laela had agreed to help as well, and even though she could not speak for the Druid elders, she volunteered to return to the heart of the Wood and try to convince them of the urgency of the situation. They were loath to become involved in the world and the ways of other men but perhaps, just perhaps, since the Elfwood itself would be affected by whatever transpired, they would lend assistance. Jaeme took her by the hand, drew her close, and spoke softly. ''My lady, whatever you and your people can do to help, you have my word that I will ever be in your debt and will devote all my energies to protect and safekeep the forest.''

Laela skipped free of the camp, and feeling the wind slip through her hair, a new freedom overcame her. She liked Jaeme and even, she supposed, the young mage, but she much preferred her own world of the Wood and always felt a sense of release when she left the outside world behind. What terrible things they did to one another out there and how deceitful they were! It was all incomprehensible to her, Druids would never act as these men did. It was impossible for them to lie or cheat or steal or harm each other in any way at all.

As she stopped in a secluded bit of brambly wood and stripped off her human clothing, she reflected on the necessity of the relationship between the People of the

Wood and the humans who lived on its fringes. Before she had been given the onerous chore, she had seldom thought about other peoples except with a shudder and the necessary effort to avoid them. She could not have imagined, would never have believed, that they could affect her Wood in any way. Now, she knew that such was not the case. She no longer had the luxury of believing her world to be inviolate, safe from the incursions of outside. The Druids of the Wood had little if any protection against things that lurked far beyond its borders, both man and monster.

She wondered if she had been given the dubious honor of ambassadress as a method of getting rid of her. It was not as though the elders believed any of what they had told her. They did not really think the position of liaison was important. What was important was to rid themselves of a nuisance. Her.

The thought rankled. But Laela had grown up enough in the few short days since she'd left the Wood to realize that she had no room for such childish emotions. If she was to protect her world, her beloved Wood, and the young lord as well, then it would be her unenviable task to convince the elders to see things as she had come to understand them. She had not told Jaeme how little the elders thought of him and his world—it would have crushed him.

She said the magic words that turned her this time into an eagle, for she could become any one of a number of forest creatures. Lewtt complained again, staying just above the treetops as his mistress swiftly climbed to the thermals and turned herself toward home. High aloft, she screamed a challenge out into the wind, her eyes, now the color of gold, fierce and bright. Let the old men beware, Laelestequenstrutia, was returning . . . girded and ready for battle.

* * *

As the army again began its march toward Castle Elfwood, Decutonius was determined to be a part of the coming confrontation. All afternoon he let his horse find its own way while he pondered and paged through his untidy collection of scrolls and potions and spells. By evening, he thought he had come on to something. Something really spectacular. A mass spell, that was the ticket! He would cast a mass spell on Jaeme's entire army, filling them with unshakable courage, fierce determination, and the strength of lions! He was so pleased with himself that he could not bear to wait until they stopped to tell Jaeme his plans. Galloping forward—a very uncomfortable and unpleasant experience, for he still was not much of a rider—he jounced up next to Jaeme, feeling his teeth and eyes rattling in his skull.

When he recovered his breath, Dec told of his plan.

Jaeme smiled and scratched his chin, but did not respond immediately. When he did, Dec was filled with chagrin. "No offense, Master Mage, but can you actually do such a thing? It sounds most difficult, casting a spell on so many people at the same time. Your magic seems to be effective, but sometimes a bit off the mark, if you know what I mean. In the interest of the safety of my men, perhaps it would be best to work with smaller numbers. It might take longer, but it would be safer."

"You think I'll bollix it up. Is that what you're trying to say?" Dec asked bitterly, his face burning crimson. Even his ears were hot, probably glowing for all he knew.

"Well, no, I mean, well, possibly . . ." Jaeme's voice trailed off as he realized that he had just insulted his mage, and anything he said to stop him would only make matters worse. "We camp one more night before we reach the castle. You may try this spell then. I don't want them all turned into rabbits or the like."

"Just have the men all together at sundown," Dec said stiffly, refusing to look at Jaeme. "We'll have a practice, like you wouldn't believe. It'll go off without a hitch. You'll see!"

Unfortunately, Dec himself had certain doubts. He had hypnotized a groundhog once and the kitchen cat who had been stalking it. Something went wrong and the groundhog had taken a fancy to him, following him everywhere for weeks before the spell wore off and it waddled back to the fields with a most confused expression on its face. The cat, on the other hand, had merely curled up and gone to sleep, waking many hours later, and had avoided Dec like the plague ever since. At least it was experience. He was older and wiser now. Back then it had been an effort several spell-levels above his expertise. Now he was a mage, even if he only held the papers of an apprentice.

He was determined to do it right. He could be a real part of this campaign, and with his assistance, Jaeme would win the battle with ease. Dec spent the remainder of the afternoon lost in a pleasant daydream wherein the spell was cast successfully, the battle fought and won; Jaeme, Polonius, and everyone in the castle were praising his brilliance and his skill; and Laela, lovely Laela, was clinging to him tightly, smothering him with kisses. Suddenly Jaeme's voice cut into his reverie.

He came to with a start, belatedly realizing that it was sundown and everyone but he had dismounted and made camp. He had been sitting in a trance atop his horse all this time. Dec flushed, hot under the collar, and quickly dismounted, feeling the ache in his buttocks and wondering for the millionth time how anyone could enjoy riding a horse.

He fussed around with his bags until the red was gone from his face, then turned to the gathered men.

"I asked for volunteers," said Jaeme with a smile. "A hundred men came forward to be imbued with magical courage. Please don't harm them." The young lord retreated quickly to the cover of some trees.

Dec faced the men, "This won't hurt a bit," he said in a squeaky high voice. There were numerous chuckles from the crowd. He frowned and lowered his voice several octaves, striding about with what he hoped was a manly gait. "What I need you to do is relax, focus on me, watch my hands, listen to the words. Most of all—and I cannot emphasize this too strongly—I need you to trust me. It is all a matter of the mind, you see."

No one looked the least bit frightened; they all stared at him with open anticipation. He was the only one who was the least bit nervous. Taking a deep breath, Dec removed a shining stone from his pocket. It was attached to a long gold chain, no thicker than a spider's web. This he began to swing back and forth at eye level, while staring out at the men and loudly and clearly reciting the rhyming words needed to weave into the spell.

Over and over he said the words, back and forth he swung the stone. Over and over, back and forth, over and over, back and forth . . . He yawned. This spell-casting really took something out of you. His eyes felt heavy, it was all but impossible to keep them open. He could hardly see the men or the stone; everything was a blur. . . .

From behind his tree Jaeme heard a distinct thump, followed by a chorus of laughter. He came back out into the clearing to find Dec lying flat on his back surrounded by a circle of laughing soldiers. Jaeme stared down at his mage and prodded him gently with his toe. Dec merely smiled goofily and puckered his lips as though he were about to kiss someone. Jaeme sighed and shook his head in disappointment. Secretly, he'd hoped that this "experiment" would actually work.

He summoned two of the men, who were still grinning from ear to ear, and directed them to carry the sleeping mage to the kitchen cart.

"Well," observed one of the men as they heaved Dec atop a sack of potatoes and turnips. "He were right about one thing. It didn't hurt a bit!"

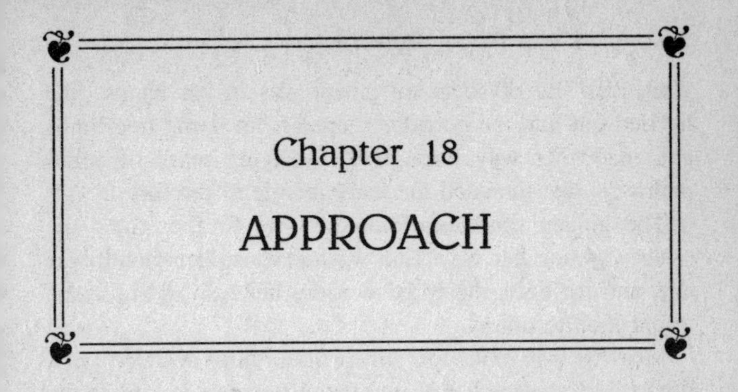

Chapter 18

APPROACH

LAELA ARRIVED IN THE HEART OF THE FOREST JUST AS NIGHT WAS falling, and whooshed through the gates past the ever watchful guardian eagles to her dressing nook. Lewtt was there to greet her as she suddenly changed back to human form.

You cut that pretty close, he remarked, chastising her for taking so long.

Laela could not have defined her relationship with the tiny sprite, but he was infinitely important to her and she relied heavily upon his opinion. Without him, she felt incomplete. She was not looking forward to the meeting with the elders and would not have wanted to go before them without Lewtt.

"Just the same, I made it." She smiled at him defiantly and held out her hand. He settled on her finger and she lifted him to her hair where he took his usual seat.

She sighed as she slipped a smock over her naked shoulders. Much as she would have liked to go straight home to her bed and burrow deep in the red and gold leaves, she knew that she could not indulge her own private wants while the fate of so many others was in her hands. She hurried out into the corridor shaped from living tree limbs and made her way through the swaying maze of aerial pathways that threaded the leafy mantle of the forest.

The golden sparkles of hundreds of fireflies lined the walls, lighting her way. She was nervous. Her mouth was dry, and for once she worried about her hair and how she might look to others.

Mistress, you look more lovely than I have ever seen you, Lewtt said, sensing her discomfort. Blowing a kiss up to the sprite's perch in her glistening curls, she took a deep breath and opened the leafy door to the council chambers.

It was dark inside; there were no fireflies here, and it took her eyes a moment to adjust. When they did, she saw, much to her surprise, the three ancients still seated upon the curved branch where she had seen them last. For all she knew, they might not have stirred at all since her last visit.

"Laelestequenstrutia," intoned the eldest of the elders as way of greeting. His voice, coming out of the near dark, sounded like dry dust rolling along the ground.

"Sir," Laela said nervously.

The old Druid rubbed his hands together and the room began to glow dim blue alternating with green.

Wise old eyes took in the sight of her. "Your time away seems to have agreed with you," mumbled the second elder, whose face, like that of his two companions, was painted dark purple. His features cracked into what might have been construed as a smile. The third elder seemed to be asleep.

It seemed strange, but could they be glad to see her? "Y-yes, sir," Laela said uncertainly.

"Why have you returned?" queried the first elder in a friendly tone. "Have you been found unsatisfactory?"

"No, sir!" Laela said. "Not at all." She was upset that

they would have so little confidence in her. "I have returned to seek your help. There is a problem."

"I told you it was a mistake to send her," the third elder said in a creaky voice without even bothering to open his eyes. "Should have sent a man!"

Laela felt her temper rising and fought to bring it under control. Send a man indeed! What could a man have done that she had not! She opened her mouth to protest, when Lewtt spoke softly to her mind, calming her, reminding her of the importance of her mission. The sprite could feel some of the Druids' thoughts. He felt sympathy there. Her job was to convince the elders of Jaeme's need, not alienate them. "Thanks, Lewtt," she whispered, thankful once again for his presence.

She took a deep breath and began again, speaking with all her persuasive abilities, using all of her wiles, including her beauty, to get the elders to listen. As she spoke, she flashed her intense green eyes first from one and then to the other. Even the elder who had been asleep, raised his eyelids for the joy of being captured by her gaze. As she finished he was listening intently.

"We have heard rumors of some of what you speak of," the first elder conceded. "It has troubled us much."

"We know what you say about the forest is true," said the third elder, his rheumy eyes still fastened on hers. "We removed all trace of the foul intruders and have done all we can to repair the damage."

"They will think twice before they enter the Wood again, won't they Laela?" the second elder muttered, pounding his fist upon his knee. "You did well, my dear. You did well." He had addressed her as Laela!

The Druidess reflected that there might have been survivors. She thought about asking what had become of them, but from the dark look on the elders' face, she quickly reconsidered.

She found herself deeply surprised by the depth of their emotion. She had always thought of the elders as barely alive, talking stick-figures, wise, and above such emotions as rage and revenge. Yet here they were acting and feeling as deeply as she did. It was amazing, and for the very first time, young Laela considered the fact that perhaps life did not truly end with the arrival of the first wrinkle.

By the time the audience ended, the third elder had begun to snore again; his feeble light had flickered and faded. Laela received the assurance that help would arrive in some form. She bowed prettily, nearly dislodging Lewtt from her curls. The blue and green glow went out, and she retreated from the room with a deep sigh of relief.

Her obligations complete, she took herself off to visit the person who meant the most to her—Myrna, the mother figure, the mentor, the wisest woman she knew, who had raised Laela when her own mother died, and taught her everything she knew.

As the owl that fluttered in through the leafy archway transformed itself into Laelesquenstrutia, she was suddenly aware that Myrna was waiting for her at the door of her private chamber, a room sweetly scented as always with innumerable bundles of flowers, herbs, roots, and leaves hanging from the ceiling. Tiny bottles, large beakers and huge cauldrons contained mysterious brews in myriad colors. Healer, mystic, white witch, spellcaster, pharmacologist—Myrna was all of those things and more.

"Oh, Myrna," cried the young girl happily as she threw herself into her mentor's arms. While old, there was strength in the thin woman's arms that belied the whiteness of her hair and quiet voice.

"Glad to see you too, dearie. My, but you look older. Life is hard beyond the forest." She was gently stroking Laela's curls.

"They're not very nice to each other out there, I'll say that." They sat down on Myrna's bed, which was made of dried leaves, and Laela related all the details of her adventures as ambassadress.

At the close of their visit, which included all the elements of any mother/daughter tête à tête—equal amounts of love and frustration stirred and brought to a boil—the two women embraced and then drew apart. Laela was now anxious to return, unable to keep her thoughts from wondering what was happening to Jaeme and whether Dec had succeeded in blowing himself up yet.

"You seem to have fallen in love with them both, haven't you?" said Myrna knowingly.

"Nonsense," Laela protested. "Why, the thought has never even crossed my mind."

"Of course not, dearie, of course not." Myrna pressed two small sacks into her palm. Laela looked at them with questioning eyes.

"It's all you'll need to help you in the coming battle," Myrna said softly, making a final attempt to smooth Laela's wild tresses back from her eyes, a futile gesture as both of them well knew.

"Will there be a battle?" Laela asked fearfully. Myrna only nodded.

"Come with me," pleaded the young girl, suddenly feeling weak and helpless. "I'm afraid. Everyone is depending on me. What if I can't do it? What if I make a mistake?"

"You'll do just fine," Myrna said soothingly, patting Laela's hand. "The elders and I have every confidence in you. Why do you think you were chosen?"

"Yes, but . . ." Laela's lower lip began to tremble.

"No *but*'s about it, you're the best we have," Myrna assured her with a smile. "I've taught you well; you will not fail us. Now, everything you'll need is in these sacks. Just rely on your instincts." Then, without looking, the old Druidess reached up and snatched Lewtt out of her hair, which he had been weaving into an awful knot. He uttered a shrill cry which echoed inside Laela's head. Myrna continued talking, uninterrupted, as she stuffed the protesting sprite into one of the sacks and pulled the drawstrings tight, tying them in a firm knot.

Laela restrained a chuckle, since Lewtt could read her thoughts. She smiled, and in obedience to Myrna's commands, said the words that turned her into a hawk which strutted proudly around on the leaf bed. Myrna gently tied the sacks, one to each leg of the hawk. That done, she stood up and the bird leapt to the old woman's outstretched arm. She walked to the door with the proud bird, testing its strong wings. There was a flutter of wings and Laela was gone into the early morning darkness.

"May the gods watch over you and protect you from harm," the old woman whispered as the hawk circled into the sky, its shrill cry wafting back to her on the cool fresh air. Then she brushed the tears from her eyes, chiding herself for being so foolish. Her little Laela had become a woman.

Lewtt struggled to free himself from the confines of the sack, but Myrna had trapped him well and good. He could feel the air rushing past, and shivered as he realized where he was. He never wanted to be above the treetops. He hollered to Laela, begging her to free him.

I'm going to be sick . . . No response.

All over these nice herbs of yours . . .

Laela just laughed. Knowing he was there for the duration, Lewtt kicked and struggled around petulantly before he settled down among the fragrant herbs, arms folded across his chest, a frown on his face. Then he remembered the knot he had woven in the old woman's hair. His little face lit up in a broad grin. Just wait till she tried to comb that out! It was the best he'd ever done!

Unable to sleep that night, Jaeme roused the camp just after midnight, anxious to move on without delay. Not a man complained, and they set out in darkness for Castle Elfwood. Well before dawn his forces crept to the banks of the River Tyrell. Castle Elfwood, a ghostly shape in the starlight, lay atop the hill to the south of them. With his goal in view. Jaeme allowed a second encampment to be formed, although no fires were permitted. In the dark in front of his tent the young Lord of Elfwood was fraught with indecision, and felt very alone. He paced back and forth, still sleepless. Old Polonius was a prisoner in the castle; Laela, whose presence and advice he had come to count on, was gone; his mage Decutonius was still lying limp on the vegetable cart; and his friend Joseph, whose advice would have been sound if simple, was away raising forces for the coming battle. Three of the sergeants of the guard sat quietly near him in the darkness, their faces all but invisible in the starlight.

At last Jaeme stopped and spoke. ''We shall not attack. We will besiege the castle and let events unfold for themselves.'' The guardsmen at his side murmured their approval. Finally he felt like sleep, and curled up on a bearskin inside his ten.

The bright summer sun was well up in the sky later that morning before Jaeme began to move. The army crossed the river upstream of the castle, with trumpets blaring. Slowly and methodically they paraded in the open field before the castle. Talvice, the new master of Elfwood watched in dismay. His carefully laid trap had obviously failed.

A stream of dark men fled from the village and poured through the castle gate. Moments later the drawbridge went up and the iron portcullis slammed to the ground.

On a silent command, contingents of footmen left the field, leaving the archers who quickly took up their positions. Those who had gone soon returned carrying logs and other bits of fence and boulders; the long, slow process of building a defensive ring around the castle had begun.

No attempt at contact was made with those within the walls. Aside from the exodus from the village, and the closing of the gate, neither side acknowledged the presence of the other. An eerie silence fell over the scene.

Atop the wall, Talvice was at first at a loss, but at length vented his wrath on Polonius, whom he called forth.

"What is the meaning of all this?" the mercenary demanded, pointing at the army now encamped around the castle. "You sent him word!"

Polonius shook his head. "There are many ways word travels in the Elfwood. You forget that the masters of this castle are also the guardians of the Wood."

Talvice fumed, again at Polonius and then at everyone else who came within his sight, accusing them all of treachery. But he was unable to prove anything.

The mercenary paced back and forth with a frown across his scarred face. Finally he sent Polonius away. "Get out of my sight, you old fool!" The master-at-arms turned silently, and disappeared down the stone stair. There was literally nothing to be done until Jaeme made a move or Felker arrived.

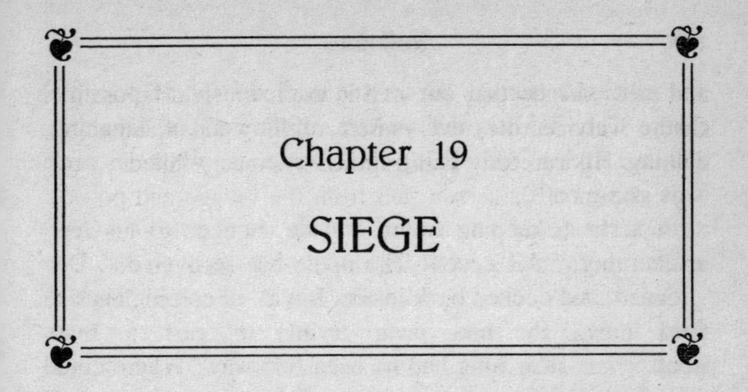

Chapter 19

SIEGE

A DAY PASSED, AND TALVICE WAS BESIDE HIMSELF. NO EMISSARY had come forth from the besieging forces and no arrow had been fired by either side. What was worse, knights, footmen, and archers from the local castles began to arrive to reinforce the besieging army. He stared down at the field from the top of the high tower and wondered just what the young whelp had in mind. He had been right when he told Penwarden not to count on a sure thing. He just wished Penwarden were here beside him now to share in his predicament.

In a small tent, at the far side of the field before the castle, a muffled groan came from within. Decutonius opened his eyes for the first time in two days. The strange surroundings disturbed him. Where was he? How did he get here? He lifted his head and surveyed the situation. He lay on a bed of straw with his arms folded across his chest. Someone had stuck a white flower in his hands as though he were lying in state. Was he alive or was he dead? There was a way to find out. He rolled over and struggled up to his hands and knees. I'm alive, he thought to himself. He crawled to the flap of the tent and peeped out as inconspicuously as possible. There were soldiers everywhere, milling about, laughing, talking, joking, sharpening their weapons. What on earth was going on?

A servant, keeping watch outside, jumped to his feet, exclaiming, "All's well! The mage has recovered!" Dec groaned, and ducked back inside. It was all coming back to him now. He had been trying to cast a mass spell. . . . How long had he been this way? Where could he hide? The flaps burst open and in swarmed servants, bringing him food and drink. Come to think of it, he was extremely hungry. After his meal, the results of his spell-casting were explained to him and he turned bright red, shooing everyone from the tent and forbidding anyone to enter without his permission. Regaining face was going to be quite a challenge.

Dec dug through his bag, found his spell books, and applied himself diligently to further study.

Late that afternoon Joseph arrived, followed by a great throng of peasants armed with pitchforks and scythes. Jaeme welcomed them gravely, thanking them personally one at a time for coming. Soon they were hard at work improving and adding to the wall of thorn bushes, spikes, and logs that was rapidly growing around the castle. Just before nightfall, a trumpet sounded atop the castle. The drawbridge came down, and four horsemen dressed in the now familiar black tunics rode out of the castle bearing a white flag and a scroll with a message. Jaeme and Joseph quickly mounted and rode to meet them. The young lord did his best to keep his expression neutral, but he dared to hope that his show of force had convinced the invaders that they could not hope to succeed.

Jaeme's hopes sank as the man bearing the scroll read the

message: "By order of our lord and master, Talvice, Duke of Frankona, and Lord of the Cillic Islands, Master of Castle Elfwood, your soldiers are hereby ordered to lay down their arms and depart from the field forthwith. By so doing, you shall avoid unnecessary bloodshed, save the village, and the lives of the prisoners held in the castle."

Joseph shook his head in disbelief, but there was more: "Furthermore, Jaeme, son of Richard Mortimer, is to renounce his claim to Castle Elfwood and swear fealty to its new master."

Jaeme had heard enough. He motioned to Joseph, and the two wheeled their mounts and rode away, even though the messenger continued to read from the scroll, ignoring the fact that he was heaping insult upon injury. At a signal from Jaeme, a group of archers closed in around the four horsemen and put arrows to their bows. On seeing this, three of the four turned and trotted back toward the safety of the castle. The reader, suddenly aware that he was alone, threw his scroll to the ground and followed his companions at a gallop.

"Here," said Jaeme to one of his best archers. "Tie this to an arrow and plant it in the flagpole atop the gate." The note read:

> To the treacherous villains inside,
>
> Release all prisoners unharmed. You and your men will be granted the honors of war. Leave Elfwood forever, and you will be allowed to return to your home with your lives and your arms.

Jaeme's face grew hard as he read it one last time, then handed it over. Moments later the arrow flew straight and true to its lofty mark. A guard above the gate quickly took the message to Talvice.

Laela, still in her guise as a hawk, arrived over Castle Elfwood well after sunup. She could see Jaeme's forces marching into position on the broad field before the castle. As she circled to land, she felt the spell begin to wear off. She had tried to go too far. She dived for the small village, spiraling lower and lower, and was about to land when the change took place and she plummeted the last several feet, landing with a crash on the thatched roof of a milk house. The thatch could have used renewing, she thought as she rubbed her bare bottom somewhat ruefully. The sack in which Lewtt was confined, now tightly attached to her ankle, jumped and quivered, and Lewtt demanded to be let out immediately.

But Laela had other concerns at the moment. She was sprawled stark naked on a village rooftop and two little girls, no more than five and seven, were staring up at her with huge eyes and open mouths. She thanked her stars that no one else had witnessed her embarrassing entrance.

"Well, don't just stand there," she commanded rather crossly. "Go and fetch me something to wear!"

The little girls did not move. The younger one regarded Laela solemnly as she placed her thumb in her mouth and then spoke around it. "Whatcha doin' up dere and whyn't you got no clothes on? Mum'd switch me, I went out widdout no clothes on." The older child said nothing at all, just clutched her pail of foaming milk and stared. Laela was beginning to feel foolish and more than a little chilled.

Her first inclination was to snap out peevishly and demand that the children obey her, but then she had another thought.

"Has either one of you ever seen a wood sprite?" she asked sweetly, ignoring the outrageous oaths that Lewtt suddenly emitted.

Just the same, the children drove a hard bargain that gained them a glittering charm, shrewd enough, even at that early age—no doubt the result of watching their parents bargain and barter on a daily basis. In due time Laela was clad in a threadbare dress that was far too large for her and only one level above being cosigned to the rag bin. Laela grasped Lewtt tightly inside the bag before she opened it, and the two girls squealed with delight when they saw him.

Awright, awright, just let me go, complained Lewtt. *But I'm not spending the night with them!* The two girls turned him upside down and pulled up his shirt and prodded his ribs. His tiny toes provided a moment of amusement when they discovered that the bottoms of his feet were ticklish. But in the end they handed him back, and it was clear that if he could not be eaten or put to work, he was of no use to them. Even at that tender age, their thoughts were centered on important issues such as food. Play had little merit.

Laela hurried toward Jaeme's fortifications, ignoring Lewtt's stormy invective and finally his stony silence. She had done what she had thought was necessary, but she realized that she could not continue to use Lewtt as a bargaining chip. She would have to think of something else, although he had been very convenient.

She found Jaeme's tent easily enough and was pleased to note how quickly he rose to his feet, spilling the mug of hot cider beside him. He stared a moment at her strange, raggedy dress, then poured out a flood of words.

"I've been worried about you. Are you well? Did it go well? What did they have to say? Is help on the way? Are you hungry?" As the bombardment of anxious questions continued, he gripped her by the wrist and seated her in his own chair. He snapped out an order, sending Skyler running for a plate of food. He handed her his own mug, not even realizing that it was empty.

She was flattered by his attentions and protested weakly that she was not hungry, although her stomach was rumbling at the thought of food. She could not remember when she had eaten last. Jaeme, and apparently his squire too, had studied her well, she realized as the platter of food arrived. Revering all animal life, she partook of no animal flesh. Arranged neatly on the plate were a variety of boiled vegetables, a chunk of fresh baked bread, and a wedge of golden cheese. There was also a tankard of still-steaming milk, and she wondered whether it had come from the little girls and if so, what it had cost.

Over the meal, they exchanged news. Laela told Jaeme what the elders had said and showed him the sacks of dried herbs. He tried his best to look impressed, but Laela could tell that he was disappointed.

"They are more than they seem, do not worry," Laela urged, remembering Myrna's curious last-minute instruction, "Wait for a prevailing wind blowing toward the castle." A cryptic command, even for Myrna, who oft handed out such puzzles to Laela. "And now, what has transpired in my absence?" she asked.

They smiled over the result of Dec's latest undertaking and tried to convince themselves that when it was needed, Dec actually would deliver as he had done with the orcs. The only real question was, What damage would he do to himself? He seemed to suffer as much as his enemies.

"It is Talvice that worries me," said Jaeme, suddenly very serious. "I am not so much concerned about us; it is the castle folk I am worried about. We have had no word whether they are alive or dead. If he has harmed them . . ."

Much later, after Laela had taken her leave of the young lord, she drew Lewtt forward on her finger and asked him sweetly to investigate and find out whether Jaeme had reason to fear for the inhabitants of the castle.

Lewtt stuck his little nose straight up into the air and turned his back on her, refusing to look at her or speak. She sighed, knowing that she deserved it, but this was too important; other people's lives were at stake. Still, sprites cared little for the larger picture and were very sensitive and took offense easily. She had some fence-mending to do if Lewtt was to cooperate.

Fortunately, Lewtt was a very soft-hearted sprite and it was hard for him to stay angry for long, especially at Laela, whom he truly adored. Teasing, tickling, cajoling and a bit of bribery, as well as kisses, worked their magic, and soon the tiny sprite was ready to do her bidding.

He was somewhat alarmed to learn that she wanted him to seek out Kizzy. Only by promising, crossing her heart backward and forward several times, and promising never, ever, to give him to another little girl, would he agree to do as she asked and find out what had transpired in the castle.

Jaeme called Joseph to his tent and told him Laela's news, but relayed second-hand, it lost much of its impact. In fact, as he repeated her words, Jaeme himself felt somewhat at a loss. What had the Druids promised? Some vague assurances of help and two sacks of dried herbs. Somehow it had seemed more important coming from Laela.

Joseph stared at him as though he had lost his mind, but kindly refrained from saying so. He cleared his throat. "Yes, well, uh, that's good, very helpful," he said. "But perhaps we should do something ourselves to aid this, uh, Druid, uh, plan.''

Jaeme could not disagree with Joseph's logic. As much as he wanted to believe that Laela's herbs would work, it was difficult. What would they do, pelt the castle with flowers? And as for Dec—he sighed inwardly—the mage was still hiding in his tent, definitely an unknown quantity. Well, maybe the young mage would be able to do something without blowing himself up, but the odds did not seem to be in his favor based upon past performance.

Joseph, always impetuous and in favor of direct action, wanted nothing less than to storm the castle walls.

``Impossible,'' Jaeme stated flatly.

``Then it is time we executed a part of your three-part plan, if you will remember,'' said Joseph. ``Let me lead a force through the tunnels and take the castle from within.'' Jaeme nodded silently, but did not at first agree. After much persuasion, however, he came round to his friend's point of view.

It was not a spectacular ploy, but Joseph knew the tunnels as well as Jaeme did. The dark corridors and the dungeons had been their playground as children. Who better to lead the attack?

``We will leave at midnight,'' Joseph said, now inspired with the notion. ``I must leave now and make my preparations.''

Later, as Jaeme sat warming his hand before the fire in front of his tent, Dec crept into the circle of light and sat morosely holding his head in his hands. Wisely, Jaeme did no more than hand him a mug of ale, sensing that the young mage would speak when he was ready.

After two mugs had been emptied Dec began to speak, a long, rambling, disjointed flow of words, and Jaeme quickly realized that these were not the first mugs Dec had indulged in that night.

The gist of the one-sided conversation was a long litany of failure, mishaps, and mischief. Dec was sunk low in his own esteem and feared that all he was really good for was the manufacture of fireballs and lightning bolts.

"Nothing wrong with fireballs and lightning bolts," Jaeme said encouragingly, trying to boost Dec's spirits. "They certainly did the trick for us against the orcs."

". . . nearly blew us all up, too," Dec mumbled, wrists hanging limply over his knees, head bowed.

"Ah, but you didn't, and that's all that matters! What splendid fireballs they were, best I've ever seen!" Jaeme declared, seeing no reason to add that he had never seen any at all until Dec's arrival. "So big, so bright—ah, so, so very fiery!" he exclaimed.

Dec's head came up slowly, and there was a look of pride in his eyes. "It was rather grand, wasn't it?" he asked tentatively.

"Grand? Why, it was the best! It was spectacular!" cried Jaeme, wondering if his father had had to do such things. He had never thought that it could be so difficult, being a lord and being responsible for people. He'd always assumed that one merely saw to it that there was enough food to eat and that things ran smoothly. He realized now that it was far more complicated than that, and shook his head over his former innocence. He was also quite aware that his father had attempted to draw him into the process on numerous occasions but that he had resisted, begging off in order to go hunting or falconing or merely running free with Joseph.

His father had let him go, standing up to Polonius' disapproval, saying that he was still just a lad and there would be plenty of time for him to learn. Jaeme knew now that Polonius had been right and his father, sadly, had been mistaken. Who could have guessed how little time would be left to them.

Suddenly, Jaeme missed his father desperately and wished more than anything that he had been more attentive, spent more time with the man who had loved him, been a better son. But he couldn't go back. The only thing left for him was to honor the memory of his father by protecting all that he had held dear, the castle itself, the Mortimer lands, and the people who depended upon the Elfwood lords to safeguard them. It was the only way he knew to prove to himself that his father's love and trust had not been misplaced.

Somehow, he found the words to inspire Dec with confidence in his own abilities. The young mage stumbled off into the darkness filled with determination to throw the best of all possible fireballs and lightning bolts. Those villains would never know what hit them!

Jaeme was still seated by the embers of the dying fire, sunk in his own dark musings, when Laela joined him with Lewtt perched on her shoulder. "Lewtt has been inside the castle," she said, causing Jaeme to sit up sharply and focus all his attention on her. "Are they well? How are they?" he asked quickly.

"Everyone, it seems, has been moved down into the lower levels, locked up in small rooms with hard doors. I'm sorry; I'm sure that isn't the right word, but it's the picture I'm getting. Lewtt had never seen anything like it before. He didn't like being there, either. It was small and dark and dirty and smelled like rotten things, he said. Kizzy was scared and cried a lot."

"The dungeons," Jaeme said grimly. "He's put them in the dungeons. No one has used them for centuries. It is a dreadful place. I was afraid of them myself as a child, although Joseph and I played down there often enough. There is nothing that can harm them, but it is far from pleasant. We will have to get them out of there as quickly as possible. Poor little Kizzy."

Later, when it was not quite dawn, Jaeme awakened in his tent. Something was nagging him, and he sat up suddenly. Then it came to him . . . If there were prisoners in the dungeon, then there were guards! He had sent Joseph and his men off, thinking that the lower levels would be empty, abandoned as they always were. He had been wrong, and now Joseph, his best friend in all the world, was advancing into a deadly trap.

Chapter 20

WAR OF WILLS

"GUARDS IN THE LOWER LEVELS!" JAEME PONDERED THE PROBLEM back and forth, trying to think of a way to warn his friend. But there was no way to get to Joseph in time. No man could now run swiftly enough to catch him.

"The sprite!" The thought came to him in a flash of inspiration. He rushed off to find Laela.

She was still half asleep, still halfway between two worlds.

Jaeme shook her gently. "Joseph must be warned. Your sprite can do it!"

Laela looked extremely dubious. Jaeme went over the logic of it a second time, thinking that she could not possibly refuse once she understood how desperate the situation was. At last Laela held up her hand to silence him. "I understand what you are saying. The problem is not with me but with Lewtt."

"What do you mean!" The earl was startled. The sprite seemed so devoted to Laela, Jaeme had not even stopped to consider that he might object.

"Lewtt doesn't like dark places, doesn't like being

underground either," she added. "He got stuck inside a badger warren when he was little. The walls collapsed on him and then the badger dug him out and nearly ate him. It was lucky that I got there in time. So you can see why he might not want to do this."

"Isn't there something we can do?" Jaeme was almost tearing his hair, worrying about Joseph and his men. He could not help but notice Lewtt's pale face peering at him through the curtain of Laela's hair. It was easy to read the sprite's fear, but there was a resolute look on the little face as well. Suddenly he spoke, unheard by Jaeme, and tugged on a curl. Laela lifted him and held him on her finger in front of her face. She cocked her head, listening, considering. She looked doubtful, shook her head, then brightened and nodded excitedly.

"Lewtt has just made a great suggestion," she said, looking at the sprite with pride, just as a mother might regard her child. Jaeme watched with interest as Laela busied herself with the two small bags Myrna had given her. She dumped the contents carefully out onto a silk cloth. More little packets and sacks. One of them seemed too light to hold anything at all.

"Oh, good. I was worried that she might have left it out," Laela said with relief. She opened the sack cautiously and Lewtt stepped off her finger and gingerly lowered himself into the opening just as one might step into a bath of cold water. Finally, even his head vanished. Laela handed a small twig down into the bag. It too disappeared from sight.

Nothing happened for a minute, and then a small, glowing object rose up out of the mouth of the sack. It was the twig, glowing like a firebrand! Lewtt followed, holding his little light aloft like a torch. He too was glowing, shimmering with light.

''Lightning-bug powder,'' Laela said. ''Takes a long time to get enough to do anything, but there's just enough to light the way for Lewtt. Go now,'' she said, tossing the sprite gently into the air. Jaeme watched spellbound as Lewtt flitted off into the sky. Bobbing up and down, he looked like a lightning bug himself, or perhaps a will-o'-the-wisp. The warning was winging its way to Joseph.

''I will not forget this,'' Jaeme said, emotion thick in his voice.

Laela was embarrassed; she scarcely knew what to say. These humans were all so extravagant with their emotions! She was spared from having to respond by a loud outcry from the guards. She and Jaeme exchanged worried glances—What now?—and then hurried toward the commotion.

The guards had surrounded a small group of men, all elderly, dressed in robes the color of the earth. They were barefoot despite the chill of the morning, and several of them wore purple or blue paint on their faces, which gave them a formidable appearance. Though they were clearly unarmed, the guards were taking no chances, holding them at spear-point and treating them as the enemy.

Laela rushed forward and positioned herself between the guards and the elders, wondering if the guards realized how lucky they were that they had not attempted to use their weapons.

''It's all right,'' she said, motioning the guards to move away. ''They're my people. Friends who have come to help.'' The guards were clearly relieved to be freed of the strange old men. There was something very spooky about them!

If the elders had been offended by the action of the guards, they gave no sign. One of them spoke.

"Greetings Laelestequenstrutia. We came as fast as we could." They began pulling small sacks and stoppered jugs out of carry-sacks. One at a time, they paused and lifted a finger to the sky or sniffed, seeming to test the wind.

"Twelve rods in that direction, I should think," said another elder, very matter-of-factly. The group dutifully padded the required distance in the direction indicated, followed at a discreet distance by a crowd of fascinated onlookers, Jaeme included.

At last they were done with their preparations. The tallest and oldest of them all, he with the purple face who appeared to be the leader, signaled Laela, and she stepped forward and dropped some of her mysterious parcels upon the ground next to theirs. Each Druid knelt on the ground behind the sack or jug he had brought. At a gesture from the leader, each untied and opened a sack, drew out the stopper in a jug. This was done with great care, taking every effort not to disturb the contents within.

Now, the open sacks and jugs lay in a line pointing directly at the castle. The leader began making motions over the vessels; words, incomprehensible words, flowed out on the night air. Many of the men watching clapped their hands over their ears, as afraid of the magic as they were of these strange men who wielded it. The other Druids were speaking now, gesturing over the sacks, and Laela, following their lead, spoke her words as well. The wind, she noted, was in the proper direction, blowing gently but directly toward the castle.

Then, even as Jaeme and hundreds of others looked on in disbelief, the unimaginable happened. Out of the little pile on the ground in front of Laela hopped a grasshopper, a large, hungry grasshopper, larger than any of the soldiers, many of whom were also farmers, had ever seen. Its large round eyes glistened eerily in the torchlight. It paused a moment, rubbing its forelegs together, and then, as Jaeme later swore, it licked its lips. There was a sudden leap and the ominous buzz of great wings as it flew off in the direction of the castle. Immediately, another grasshopper emerged from the pile and did the same. And it was followed by two grasshoppers who were even larger.

Incredulous eyes watched as all the sacks and jugs began to wriggle and writhe, emptying themselves of their contents. What had once been mixtures of dry powders, flaked leaves, and bits of herbs were now long, waving columns of ants, roaches, silverfish, weevils, worms, shrews, voles, mice, rats, bats, and birds. The wall of besieging soldiers parted anxiously in the face of the writhing plague of vermin that was descending upon the unsuspecting castle, and—more to the point—it's supplies of food. Soon shrieks and cries could be heard from within the walls. Horses could be heard running loose, and more yells and shouts echoed back and forth. Fires sprang up, and presently great clouds of smoke poured up from behind the walls. Jaeme shuddered to think what was going on inside.

The horde of horrors that the Druids had unleashed upon the castle set about their work with ruthless efficiency. Doing exactly what they had been instructed to do, they set upon whatever foodstuffs they were able to find. Bales of hay, salted loins of pork, smoked racks of venison, rounds of waxed cheese, barrels of milled oats and flours—every bit of food down to the smallest pinch of seasoning was soon crawling with life.

The plague was discovered by the scullery maids, always the first to rise. Every available hand and foot was soon set to squashing, smashing, sweeping, picking, and wiping. But it did no good whatsoever—the numbers of crawling, flying, wriggling creatures appeared to be legion, and no sooner was one killed than two more took its place. Horses in the stable broke loose and ran amok. Talvice ordered fires set to destroy the vermin, but this merely made things worse for the humans.

By noon, not one shred of food for beast or man was left inside the castle. It had all been consumed, chewed, swallowed, licked, masticated, and devoured by the strange plague. Even more mysterious was the manner in which the creatures departed. When the last crumb of bread in the pantry had entered the last gullet, the last trace of flour sucked from the bottom of the barrel, the last strand of hay cheerfully chewed into grasshopper hors d'oeuvres, every single insect, invertebrate, mouse, vole, shrew, bat, rat, and bird vanished in the blink of an eye.

The besieging soldiers were not the only ones who watched the spectacle of the plague in awe. Hearing the noise, Dec had emerged from his tent and had stood dumfounded as the swarm rolled across the field, up the walls, and into the castle. Now that was magic! Fortunately, Dec was still rather naive and unworldly. Another mage might have fallen into a grand funk over the Druids' skill, or passed it off as nothing. Once the infestation was in full swing, he made his way through the crowds of onlookers to where Laela still knelt with the other Druids. It appeared to him that they were finished.

"That was really incredible!" He stammered, "I mean, I've never seen anything like that before. Do you think you could teach me how you did that, or is it like, a secret?" He almost swallowed his tongue as the tallest purple-faced elder swung around to face him. Only then did it occur to him that perhaps there was some sort of protocol which he should have followed. It was easy to see that they were not ordinary folk; perhaps he was wrong in even speaking to them. He gulped loudly and began to walk backwards, stammering out his apologies.

Laela was praying for the earth to open up and swallow her, when to her astonishment the elder crooked his finger and beckoned the young mage toward him. Dec obeyed, walking as slowly as if he were to be put to death. The old Druid put his hand on the boy's shoulder, and the two of them walked apart, heading for the small wood that bordered the field.

No one ever knew what they talked about. Dec never spoke of it. And Laela was not young enough or foolish enough to ask the elder. But by evening, when the old man returned with Dec, and the others had gathered up their now empty sacks and jugs and walked back the way they had come, they left a much different Decutonius than the one they had found.

Apprehension and self-doubt were gone, and in their place was a quiet aura of confidence and competence that was apparent to anyone who spoke to him. He strode off to his tent with an air of purpose that was amazing to behold. Not once did he trip on his robes, and when he bid a soldier good night, the stammer was gone from his voice.

After the strange yet impressive departure of the Druid elders and Dec, Jaeme called Laela to him.

"I know you have been busy all day, but I must know," he said, a worried expression on his face.

She anticipated his question. "Lewtt arrived in time. They await your command to attempt to break in. Joseph and his men lurk behind closed doors."

"Thank you, Laela," he said, smiling now. "That is good news indeed."

It was nearly dawn the next day when Dec arrived outside Jaeme's tent and insisted on seeing the lord. Skyler was adamant and refused him entry. Jaeme, who had been unable to sleep, heard the exchange.

"It's all right, Skyler," he said. "I am awake. Let the mage enter."

Jaeme was actually glad to have something to listen to other than his own thoughts, which had been troubling him for hours.

"I have it," Dec said calmly as he sat down on the floor next to Jaeme.

"It?"

"I know what to do now," he said quietly, and with his newfound assurance, he began to outline the course of action to Jaeme. When he was finished, Jaeme was in agreement with him.

"By all means give it a try. I'm told that they're out of food now, and if your spell works, they may sally forth to their deaths this very day."

"Or just plain surrender," added Dec.

"Much the preferable option," Jaeme agreed.

The two left the tent with Skyler in tow. It was still dark outside, but a faint glimmer of dawn could be seen crawling up at the horizon. It was the darkest hour of the night, the time when even the owl and the other hunters of the night are abed. The three came to the wall of logs that had been thrown up around the castle. The men on guard greeted them in silent amazement.

"I must go the rest of the way alone," the young man whispered. Jaeme shook his hand. Then, with his newfound agility, Dec crept over the barricade, across the narrow gap between it and the castle wall, and right up to the river's edge. Jaeme was not sure what he saw, but it appeared as though Dec simply floated across the rushing water, and fastened himself somehow to the rocks at the base of the wall.

Good, Dec thought as he landed gently on the far bank of the river. He had remembered his teleport spell well. Now for the important bit of magic. Slowly he began to recite the words he had spent the night committing to memory. There was no sign from the castle that his presence had been detected, and when he was done, he gave a gentle leap, floated effortlessly back across the river to the bank, and slipped back to camp as silently as he had left.

"Done?" Jaeme whispered anxiously.

"Done," Dec confirmed. His face was drawn and his eyes looked very tired. "Took a lot out of me though!"

"There was no . . . ?"

"No, no problem," Dec answered with a gentle smile, not in the least offended that Jaeme had doubted his abilities. "I need to sit." Dec plopped down to the ground. Skyler brought him a drink of water.

"Thanks," said the mage, and then he slurped the whole cup empty. "Everything will go exactly as planned. Unless I miss my guess, they will all be overcome with despair."

"And the prisoners?" asked Jaeme worridly.

"Them too, I fear," Dec replied. "But if Talvice thinks his situation is hopeless, he must soon surrender. And even if he remains set against us, his men will question themselves and their leader. They will be possessed by an overwhelming desire to give up."

"If it works as you say, then we can retake the castle with no loss of life!" Jaeme said with wonder.

* * *

Had it not been for the resounding echoes of the empty pantries, the hollow reverberation of the flour barrels, the vacant hayloft above the stable, it could all have been a terrible dream. The reality was worse. They were now without provisions and without the means to resupply, for the entire castle was surrounded by an ever-growing army. Talvice's once invincible position had now become far less secure. When he had arrived, there had been enough food and fodder to carry them through an extended seige. Now there wasn't enough to sustain a hungry ant.

Needless to say, Talvice was less than pleased. In fact, he was downright testy. Even the bravest and the most foolhardy of his men knew enough to stay away. He paced back and forth in the high tower, looking out at the enemy who had been joined by yet another contingent of men—ragtag farmers, from the look of them, but the scythes they carried glinted in the early morning light, speaking eloquently of frequent honings, and their pitchforks had evil points capable of skewering a man, ripping through his belly, pulling his innards . . . no! NO!

Now even he was doing it! What was this mindless despair that overwhelmed him? Talvice stormed down the stair, past a pair of guards who lay cringing in terror by the door. He stopped and looked at them in disbelief. Some terrible magic no doubt, much like that infernal plague set upon him. Talvice set out for the wall overlooking the field. He would show them! He'd show them that Talvice was better, stronger, tougher than anyone could imagine! He would not fall for their tricks or run from them and their packs of rats!

Talvice strode out of the tower and summoned up Polonius, whom he was no longer attempting to convince of his legitimacy. His guards all cringed at their posts, so he personally dragged Polonius out of his bed and up onto the wall, where he all but tossed the old man over the edge of the rampart and commanded him to call Jaeme.

Polonius hailed the army below, and soon enough, Jaeme rode bravely forth, mounted upon Firebrand. Behind him, on foot, came Dec, Laela, and Andrew the smith. They stopped within easy hail of the castle, seemingly unconcerned for their safety.

The earl was distressed at Polonius' condition. The old man's beard hung down in tatters, his hair was disheveled and unwashed, his skin was a sickly yellowish-grey. Jaeme was shaken, but knowing how much depended on appearances, he was careful not to show his dismay. He held his silence, refusing to call up to the castle, forcing Talvice to speak first.

Speak Talvice did, although rant would have been a better term. "You won't drive me out! I won't go! I'll never leave!" he screamed, spittle flecking his lips and chain mail. Desperation was in his eyes.

"Do your worst!" he railed. "I'll be here till I rot!" Perhaps realizing what he had said, he changed his tactic. "Lay down your arms!" he demanded unexpectedly. "Surrender to me immediately!"

"Release the hostages, and I will be glad to consider your request," Jaeme called back coolly.

"Release the hostages?" Talvice was wild with anger. "YOU do as I say or I'll release the hostages, all right! I'll release them one at a time—by catapult—and their deaths will be on your soul!"

Jaeme blanched and was on the verge of speaking, when Dec walked up to him quickly, reached up, and touched his arm. The earl bent over and listened as Dec whispered something into his ear. Jaeme sat up in the saddle suddenly.

"Are you absolutely sure you can do it?" he asked.

"Been doin' it since I was an infant," came the confident reply. There was something in the young mage's eyes that gave Jaeme the courage to defy this last desperate gamble Talvice was taking.

"Life on the borderlands is always at risk," Jaeme called out boldly. "I must do as I must, as will you. Let this remain between the two of us. Do not use helpless pawns as bargaining chips. It is beneath honor. It does not suit even you."

"Do not speak to me of honor! Speak only when you are ready to surrender!" screamed Talvice. He yanked Polonius backward by the neck of his robes and the two of them vanished from the ramparts.

"Stand ready to do you work, mage," Jaeme instructed. "For I know not in which direction he shall be firing."

Laela suddenly grasped what was about to happen. "You can't do this," she pleaded. "They will be killed."

"Have faith in our mage," said Jaeme. Laela stared at him incredulously.

"Listen," began Dec hurriedly. "We haven't much time. Here's what I want you all to do . . ."

Instructions were quickly passed among the soldiers who were gathered round, and Dec prepared himself, taking deep breaths.

Moments later a deep *thwack* came from within the castle walls, followed immediately by a terrifying scream. Up over the wall flew Polonius, waving his arms and legs helplessly all the while cursing Talvice to eternal doom. Those behind the barricades set up a great wail. The body of the master-at-arms seemingly crashed to the ground, and a group of soldiers rushed forward and carried his limp body away.

Talvice reappeared atop the wall. "There are more to come," he screamed insanely. "Do you yield?"

Jaeme sat stone-faced upon his horse and made no answer.

"Again!" Talvice screamed, signaling to his men below. He had managed to coerce a few of the braver ones back into action.

There was another wooden *thwack* and a scream, and a small boy came flying over the wall, kicking and screaming bloody murder. He too landed amid a shriek from the onlookers, and his body was quickly carried off.

The now insane laughter of Talvice floated down from the castle ramparts. Now, at regular intervals, helpless, flailing hostages flew out over the walls like huge hailstones, crashing down one after the other, and each new body was met with cries of grief.

As each victim neared the ground, however, Dec concentrated intensely, and levitated the terrified person at the last moment before the fall would result in death. Visually the effect was startling, and most of the men who watched were convinced that all who had been thrown over the walls were dead. But so far, Dec had managed to save them. Apparently Talvice had only been able to man one of his catapults, which had worked in Dec's favor. He shuddered to think what he would do if more than one body came flying over the wall at once.

In this way all that were thrown, more than half the women and children, were already rescued. Talvice, however, seeing that his gambit had failed, despaired at the lack of success. He had been so sure that the young lord would give in, that he would not have the iron will necessary to watch his people being slain. Yet the young lord had stood there silently and watched his own people die.

Talvice screeched. How could he have been so wrong! The black mood descended on him even further. He had failed. If he kept this foolishness up he would have no hostages left! He ordered the catapult to stop.

Chapter 21
THE DUEL

IT WAS NO LONGER POSSIBLE FOR TALVICE TO CONVINCE HIMSELF that victory was within his grasp. The castle was surrounded by numbers superior to his own, his supply of food was nonexistent, and almost all his men were overcome by despair. And the despair coursed through his every fibre too.

Now came the final blow. He watched in disbelief as Felker's army rode into Jaeme's camp and took up positions alongside the besiegers. For a brief moment Talvice had hoped that Felker would turn the tide, would attack Jaeme from within, but Felker's men joined Jaeme's at the barricade. It appeared that Felker had observed the gauge of the wind, had decided to cut his losses and side with Jaeme. Talvice gnashed his teeth in rage.

''So, the blackguard would leave me to die alone, would he,'' Talvice said under his breath. ''Well, I'll have something to say about that!''

Nor would he accept his defeat so easily. There was still a slim chance. . . . Hurrying to the nearest crenelation on the walls he called down to Jaeme, now demanding a man-to-man confrontation, swords and shields, combat between the two of them with no magic, no extraordinary assistance, winner take all. Talvice was betting everything on Jaeme's inexperience, his inability to face a thrown gauntlet without picking it up.

If Jaeme accepted the challenge he would soon learn, as Talvice had, that there were times when appearing the coward was far preferable to certain death.

Dec and Laela did their best to dissuade Jaeme from accepting Talvice's challenge. Jaeme himself was not eager to accept, but he was tired of the whole affair and was ready to make an end of it. He tried to explain the situation to his friends. "Don't you see, if we can settle it, between the two of us, it means that many others will be spared from death." Laela and Dec did not look convinced.

"This is the way it should be," Jaeme insisted. "Wars ought to be settled between the two warring principals without dragging innocents into an affair they had no part in the making of. Think how much hardship it would cause if even one man were killed. What would become of his family?"

"Many already lie dead. And what part did you have in the making of this matter?" Laela snapped. "I don't recall that you had anything to do with starting this fight!"

"You think it will cause a great hardship if but a single farmer is killed?" asked Dec.

Jaeme nodded.

"Well, think how much hardship will be caused if YOU get killed. Everything would go to pieces, and if you think Talvice would give a rat's tail about the hardship of the people, you've got a lot to learn. No one, certainly not your people, can afford for you to risk your life in individual combat. Say no. We'll think of something else."

But even though Jaeme did as Dec asked and pondered the issue, the more he thought about it, the more unfair it seemed to have others risk their lives for what was essentially his honor and his birthright. Against the backdrop of a chorus of groans, Jaeme turned in the saddle and yelled up to Talvice.

"Your challenge is accepted!"

"Call off your magicians. This will be a fair fight!" came the reply.

"Done! Let us meet on the drawbridge. To the winner goes the castle!" Jaeme rode forward slowly, followed by his retinue, all of whom dispaired of his surviving the coming duel.

The portcullis clanked up slowly, and apparently someone had chopped the ropes to the drawbridge, for it came roaring down too fast and smashed onto the opposite bank in a cloud of dust.

Talvice appeared at the gate, flanked by a few of his men, all of whom bore terrified expressions. They were there in name only. The mercenary wore no helm, but carried a large round black shield emblazoned with a yellow diamond. In his other hand he held out a drawn long-sword.

The young Lord of Elfwood dismounted, and Skyler ran up to him with a large green kite shield. A shield that was a good deal larger than the one carried by Talvice, but also heavier and more ungainly. Jaeme drew his sword, the one given him by his father posthumously through Polonius. Suddenly it occurred to him that apart from lopping off the head of a sleeping orc, he had never used this blade in combat. He prayed it was as good and true a weapon as it looked and felt.

They advanced upon each other slowly, then stopped,

facing each other at the middle of the bridge. All had fallen silent, and the gentle rustle of the waters of the River Tyrell rushed pleasantly beneath them in wry contrast to the seriousness of the business above. Then Talvice raised his sword and let out an oath.

"You shall die, young fool!" he called, and lunged forward swinging. The young lord stepped back smartly and met the blow with his upraised shield. A deep clang of steel shattered the silence. The force of the impact stung Jaeme's arm and drove him back two steps. He recovered his balance, and his sword suddenly took on a life of its own, thrusting forward at an opening Talvice had left. The blade was going for his heart, and Jaeme could feel its intent. Almost too late, Talvice turned the point away with his weapon, and instead of delivering a death blow, the tip only ripped the cloth from his shoulder. Now they circled, and their swords began to clash together with a deadly regularity, percussive rhythm of battle that must surely end in one of their deaths.

Jaeme may have agreed to the conditions of the battle, but neither Dec nor Laela had. Watching anxiously from the top of a tree, Dec did his best to aid Jaeme with his magic, but no matter what he did, his spells all seemed to fail. There was no way that he could have known that Gratten, under orders from Felker, was hard at work close by, countering his every move. So, in a sense, two duels were being fought at the same time. The net result was that the sword fight on the bridge was indeed being fought unassisted.

The drawback to this interference, which Felker had considered and then dismissed, was that while Gratten was occupied with Dec, he could not use his magic to influence the outcome of the battle either. But so certain was Felker of

Talvice's winning, that he was not overly concerned. Still he watched the battle carefully. He was impressed with the swordsmanship of young Jaeme. If anything, he was better than his father had been.

Laela was equally distressed by Jaeme's decision, and while there was little that she could do to help or hinder the battle, there was something else she could do. She slipped away from the tree that held Dec and dropped out of sight behind the barricade. Shedding her clothing, she quickly said the words that transformed her into her soul mate, the falcon. Her screeching went unheard as all eyes and ears were glued to the battle at the gate. Rising swiftly to avoid a random arrow, she crossed over the wall and dived into the tower of the castle, spiraling effortlessly down the stairs, through the Great Hall, and landed with a flutter in the empty kitchens. Turning her head quickly from side to side, she searched for the way to the dungeons. The falcon that was Laela strutted cautiously down into the scullery, totally unnoticed, for all the guards had left their posts. She transformed herself back to human form, and wrapped herself as best she could in some rags. The doorway leading down to the dungeon stood open. She inched slowly down the dark stairway that led to the lowest levels.

Here too, the guards were so completely demoralized that they merely watched as she relieved them of their keys and systematically opened all the doors to the cells. Soon the freed prisoners were busy releasing the others. That done, the freed hostages seized their former captors and threw them in the cells they had occupied only moments before, and turned the keys in the locks. This was the last straw for many of the burly soldiers, who broke down and wept, totally unaccustomed to defeat.

After that, it was but a simple matter to find the hidden doors and open them for Joseph and his men. Lewtt telepathically guided Laela to the door behind which he waited, still covered in the luminescent dust and seated on top of Joseph's head. The sprite was delighted at being freed from the dark, dank tunnel, and lost no time in situating himself deep in Laela's curls. She praised Lewtt effusively, and while he preened and reveled in her praise, she doubted he would allow himself to be persuaded to do such a disagreeable thing again.

Outside, the battle raged on. First Talvice would bear down on Jaeme, driving him back with his greater weight and strength, and then Jaeme, parrying the thrusts with his natural, lithe grace, would, with the aid of the magic in his sword, attack his opponent with telling thrusts of his own.

For a while, there was no clear victor. Each time Talvice drove Jaeme back, the young lord managed to circle around and fight his way back. The sword given him by his father seemed to be keeping Jaeme alive. Not for nothing had he and Joseph and their friends spent all those long hours in furious mock battle. But talented as he was, he lacked the experience that lurked behind the fell blows struck again and again by Talvice.

Suddenly Jaeme misstepped and the tip of Talvice's sword slashed across his shoulder, drawing blood. A shudder rose up from the crowd. The young lord gritted his teeth. He dared not forget that the fate of his home, his lands, and his people rested upon the outcome of the battle. He must not lose!

Talvice, however, had equally strong stakes in the fight. The life of a mercenary was often short, and offered few long-term rewards. Talvice was not yet old, still in the prime of his manhood, but he could feel the ache and pull of his muscles now. Jaeme was testing him to his limits.

Castle Elfwood suited his needs exactly. It was isolated enough that he would not have to be guarding his back at all times. This was what he wanted and he was determined to win it. He could envision years of profitable, leisurely raiding whenever the larder or purse demanded, or when boredom set in.

The battle had already taken far longer than Talvice would have preferred. He was half a head taller than Jaeme and was easily double his weight, most of it heavy muscle, which added to the power of his blows but was difficult to sustain in extended battle.

Talvice's usual method of combat was to get in as quickly as possible, overwhelming the enemy with sheer strength and fury. It had not worked this time. The young lord was uncommonly skillful and his sword seemed to parry and thrust with uncanny speed. From the ease with which the youngster handled it, it had to be far lighter than Talvice's own blade, yet it was strong enough to strike sparks when the two blades clashed. Talvice was determined to win the blade for his own. And, once it was, he would plunge it into Jaeme's heart.

Both men had slowed now and they were drenched with sweat, obviously tiring. The field was generally silent except for the occasional roar at a near miss or an exceptionally well done parry of a thrust. Neither the soldiers of Talvice, who now lined the walls, nor the men who grasped the rough barricade, dared take their eyes from the field or wager upon the outcome. All realized that their lives hung in the balance.

The tension was mounting, all but unbearable, a palpable force pressing in on all sides, and still there was no predictable victor. And then things changed. Talvice suddenly noted an opening that Jaeme left each time he parried a high slash. The mercenary faked the slash, Jaeme moved, and Talvice kicked with his foot, hitting the young man full force in the groin. Jaeme howled, doubled over, and fell to one knee, sword wedged in the earth.

Talvice, using his advantage, lost no time in striking Jaeme on the head with the butt of his sword, knocking his opponent to the ground. Those gathered behind the barricade cried out with a single anguished voice, and for one horrible moment, it seemed that all was lost.

However, instead of striking, Talvice leaned on his sword, drawing in great breaths, badly winded and needing time to recoup before he could deal the final blow. It was cruelly apparent to all those who watched that the older man had been at the very end of his strength, and had Jaeme been but able to hold out a moment longer, it might have been Talvice lying half-conscious on the ground about to die.

Jaeme moved his head slowly, and clumsily struggled to his knees, still stunned by the impact. Dec watched in horror. All was lost. Not even Jaeme and his wonderful sword could recover in time to deal with Talvice. But still, Talvice did not strike.

"I have something to tell you," the mercenary gasped in a low voice that could be heard only by those who stood closest, "before you die, you young fool . . ."

Felker, who waited in mortal fear of just such words, let out a battle cry and rushed forward from the ranks of the defenders, bearing down on Talvice swiftly with sword drawn. It happened so fast that scarcely anyone realized what was happening until it was over. Felker came on like a madman, almost a blur to the eyes. Coming up behind Talvice, Felker plunged his sword into the man's back, driving it through his body with all the strength he possessed. He let go his blade and exclaimed:

"Die, you vile murderer of Richard!"

Talvice, too, had dropped to his knees, Felker's sword full through his body, blood streaming down from the grievous wounds, and still he lived. Perhaps the blade missed his heart, or perhaps hatred fueled him when he realized who had struck him down. Whatever the reason, Talvice rose unsteadily to his feet, and his own sword still in hand, advanced upon Felker. There was no courage in the master of Harrowhall now, for he was facing the walking dead, yet he stood his ground transfixed. Talvice swung his own blade and sliced Felker across the upper body. Had he not been mortally wounded, his blow would certainly have killed Felker.

Talvice raised his sword for yet another blow.

It was at that moment that Gratten threw a desperate spell. Dec, and Laela, who by now had returned from within, both saw the Red Mage work his magic, but they stayed their hand. Not wishing to aid Talvice, they did nothing to impede the villainous magician.

Talvice let out a terrible cry, covering his eyes with his hands and stumbling around blindly. Felker lost no time. He seized the man's own bloody sword, and with a mighty swing, lopped the mercenary's head clear off his body. It bounded with a sick thud to the ground, and then the body fell, like a mighty oak. Talvice was at last dead.

It was all over. Felker was the first to reach Jaeme, raising him from the ground. "No need to worry, my lord. I have killed the dastardly intruder myself," he said in an unctuous tone, seemingly taking credit for the entire battle by merit of his single black deed. Jaeme stared up at him speculatively, too dazed to speak, still shocked by what he had just witnessed. Soon Jaeme was surrounded by friends and landsmen. A great hurrah spread across the armies arrayed in the field.

A week later much had been restored to normal. Jaeme's head had cleared, and most of his wounds were healed. The mercenaries had been sent back across the sea to the continent, and life in Castle Elfwood had almost returned to everyday routine. Felker, as usual, managed to explain away the actions of his men, attributing them to the evil works of Talvice, and was thus forgiven.

Now Jaeme, Polonius, Dec, Laela, Joseph, Andrew, and the children Kirk and Kizzy, were seated around an oaken table on the dias in the Great Hall, enjoying a meal of smoked ham and mead. The rest of the smoke-filled hall was bustling with merrymakers from the surrounding lands and castles. Wine flowed like water, and an unending stream of servants carried in trays heaped with all manner of food. The castle had been amply reprovisioned, largely from Felker's own larder, a gift which Jaeme had not refused. Felker was in attendance, seated at one of the lower tables. Jaeme caught his eye, and the Lord of Harrowhall raised a cup to the Lord of Elfwood.

"I wonder if we'll ever know what part Felker played in all of this," Jaeme murmured.

"I never trusted the man," Polonius said, pressing his lips together. "Your father told me I was being uncharitable, but there is something about the fellow that sets my teeth on edge."

"He'll bear watching," Jaeme agreed. "We will not be taken unawares again."

"I was not for a moment taken in by that ruffian Talvice's claim that he had been sent by Edmund." Polonius sniffed disdainfully. "Why, I saw through his plan straightaway. Did he think that he was dealing with a country boob? Really!"

Everyone carefully hid their smiles from the old man, who had been instructed by the castle healer to take things very slowly for a while.

"Why, thank you, dear. I could have gotten that myself, but thank you." Polonius took the refilled goblet from Laela, who smiled at him prettily and curtseyed. "As I was saying . . ."

Polonius continued for some time, but the others managed to have their say as well, including Lewtt, even though he was perched in Kizzy's lap and enduring having his hair tied in knots by the little girl's now experienced fingers. He had discovered that it was quite pleasant having two big people to talk to, and in some ways Joseph was much nicer than Laela, who could shut him out any time she wanted. Joseph had no such magic means.

Jaeme watched the small gathering of friends, his own small family, as they ate and drank and bickered pleasantly, rehashing the recent events, each of them remembering the story in his or her own way. He felt warm inside for the first time in a long while. All was safe now, for the time being, and with the help of such loyal friends, Castle Elfwood and the ancient forest it was sworn to protect would remain safe.

Jaeme knew that there would always be others who were greedy for personal gain and not hesitant to call upon the powers of darkness to aid them in their quest. But he had gained a certain confidence that he hadn't had before. He could face any challenge with friends such as these.

Laela looked up just then and caught his eye. Slowly, she

raised her cup. Dec did so as well, and the three friends toasted each other, silently renewing their vows of friendship, trust, and honor. They were the guardians, and as long as they lived, so would Castle Elfwood and the ancient forest.